The
BACK PAGE

BY JACK DOUGLAS MITCHELL

A COLLECTION OF STORIES
FROM THE AMERICAN HUNTER MAGAZINE

ILLUSTRATIONS BY HARRY LLOYD JAECKS

BOOK SERVICE

For information address the National Rifle Association,
1600 Rhode Island Avenue, N.W., Washington, D.C. 20036
ISBN 0-935998-44-6
Library of Congress Catalog Card Number 82-62010
Published March, 1983
Second Printing, May, 1990

Printed in the United States

Jacket cover painting by Bob Kuhn

Book illustrations by Harry Lloyd Jaecks

Illustration on jacket flap and back cover by Tom Beecham

Published by the
National Rifle Association of America
1600 Rhode Island Avenue, N.W.
Washington, D.C. 20036

George Martin, Executive Director, NRA Publications
Frank A. Engelhardt, Dep. Director & Book Service Manager
Michael A. Fay, Manufacturing Director
Harry L. Jaecks, Art Director

DEDICATION

*"To my hunting and fishing friends
and to my wife, Ruby,
who seems to understand us."*

INTRODUCTION

I have known Jack Mitchell for a long, long time. And, for as long as I have known him I have looked forward to this book. Before there was a "Back Page," or before there was a magazine titled the AMERICAN HUNTER for that matter, Jack's stories about hunting cronies, bird watchers, dogs both good and not so good, guns, shots made, shots missed, and his various encounters with elements of the gunning life experienced in coverts as near as over-yonder and as far off as the Himalayas have been personal high spots of shared, memorable hunting camps and forgettable convention hospitality suites.

During his years as advertising mogul for Remington Arms Company, corporate demands encroached deeply upon his free time afield with gun and/or rod. To this day Jack remains capable of making this declaration without a hint of a smile, which is testimony to his abundant abilities as an ad man. Consequently, there never seemed to be enough time for him to hunker behind a typewriter and polish, and often as not, make his stories suitable for one printed page of a family magazine.

It was early in the festivities of his retirement party, held appropriately at Weston Gun Club, that we first discussed the possibility of his writing what was to become known as "The Back Page" on a monthly basis. It must have been early in the evening because the tag hours are rather jumbled and vague to the memory. However, rational discussions took place over the next several weeks. Jack was like a Lab puppy encountering crust-ice for the first time. He wanted to plunge in but was hesitant to make the jump. So, metaphorically and very nearly actually, according to his wife Ruby, he bounced up and down the shoreline and barked. First he barked at deadlines, which was a hollow concern. For now, according to the editors, deadlines concern him not at all. Then he barked at the length of copy required; then at the proposed subject matter. But, finally, he made the plunge.

It was the September 1978 issue of AMERICAN HUNTER that carried the very first "Back Page" by Jack Douglas Mitchell. It introduced us to a very special man with an exceptional understanding of the hunter's lifestyle and values. A man with the unique talent to express feelings that make us laugh a little, cry a little, and which remind us to slow down just a bit to appreciate the obvious but all too often overlooked. Jack allows us to see our frailties and those of others for what they are. In a very real sense, he causes us to examine and appraise our real, gut-level values.

We are told that one of the criteria for achieving "classic" status is a book's rereadability. If ever a book should become a classic, then this one should. Every Jack Mitchell story bears repeated reading. I intend to do just that and invite you to join me.

GEORGE MARTIN
Executive Director, N.R.A. Publications

THE DRAWINGS

This book is as much about feelings as anything else. Those many and varied feelings experienced by hunters which Jack Mitchell has the gift of insight and perceptiveness to absorb and then recount in a manner that all readers, regardless of age or experience, relate to.

The task of visualizing and rendering the illustrations that blend with and complement such restated feelings requires a particular talent. That talent is exhibited in the drawings of Harry Lloyd Jaecks shown on these pages.

Harry's obvious feel for outdoor and wildlife subjects comes from a life-long experience in the out-of-doors and in the sketching of things natural. Although his business hours are spent as the Divisional Art Director for NRA Publications, his "off" hours are spent successfully satisfying his desire to compose fine art creations with outdoor/wildlife/nature themes.

In the years to come, sporting art buffs will have learned to recognize and value the work of this fine young artist.

CONTENTS

1 THE OWL HOOTED FIVE TIMES

THE far-off voice of an owl, like the baying of a distant hound, floated out of the swamp and across the moonlit lawn to where the two old men sat quietly rocking on the porch of the big white house. Both the rocking chairs creaked to a halt and, after a pause, one of the men said, "Listen to that old hoot owl."

"It isn't a *hoot* owl," the other man said. "It's a great *horned* owl. He's a five-noter. You can count 'em."

As if instructed, the owl responded with five deep and resonant hoots. "Five," the hoot owl man counted. "It's a male. The female usually goes about six to eight hoots."

"If you know that much about owls, how come you called him a *hoot* owl. There's no such bird," the horned owl man said.

"Called him that when I was a kid, I guess—and maybe just to get a rise out of you. You aren't exactly talkative, you know," the other man said.

"Sorry, Mr. Lawson, guess I just haven't found anybody around this place worth talking to. You're the new one aren't you?"

"Yep—two days ago. And by the way, the name is Dawson, not Lawson. Jed Dawson."

"Pleased to meet you, Mr. Dawson. My name is Wilton. Luke Wilton."

"How long you been here, Mr. Wilton?"

"Forever," Luke answered.

"Is it that bad?" Jed asked. "My nephew called it a Senior Citizens Center, but it looks like an old folks home to me. Pretty

1

nice though. Out here in the country. Don't care much for cities."

"Me neither," Luke said, and they went back to rocking. The owl, having served to introduce the two men, was no longer heard.

The moon rose slowly over the silent woods. "Wouldn't be a bad night to go coon hunting," Jed finally said.

"Too dry," Luke grunted. "Need rain."

They rocked on steadily until Luke asked, "Do much hunting?"

"Quite a bit," Jed said. "Why?"

"Well, I was beginning to believe that the only people they let in this place were golfers and bowlers."

"My brother used to play golf," Jed said.

"Hope he got over it," Luke said with another grunt.

"You're not very tolerant, are you?" Jed said.

"Nope. Can't afford the time. Last fellow I mentioned hunting to around here told me all about mutual funds and how his bowling team won the company trophy," Luke said. "What kinds of hounds did you run?"

"Most kinds. Like redbones and black and tans on coon. Walkers on fox."

"Don't like Walkers."

"Why not?"

"Look too much like a pointer. Ever see a Walker and a pointer coming down the road? Same action. Same hard head."

"Ever own a pointer?" Jed asked.

"Nope. They'll hunt for anybody with a gun. I want my own dog—a setter."

"Well, that settles that," Jed said, and went back to rocking.

"Nothing prettier," Luke said.

"Than what?" Jed asked.

"A litter of setter pups. You end up wanting to keep 'em all. Why, one time we had this little runt of a pup named Sam, and my Mary . . ."

Luke's voice trailed off, and he started to rock again, harder than ever, as he stared off into the moonlit night. Jed, sensing what was happening to Luke, broke in and said, "My nephew and his little boy are coming out to visit next Sunday, and they may bring our new pointer pup. He's about six months old now."

"Time to start training him," Luke said quietly.

2   "That's just it," Jed said. "They haven't got the time, and I've

been thinking of trying to do it myself, now that I'm feeling better. I can still walk pretty good. How about you?"

"What *about* me"? Luke said with a scowl.

"Can you still walk—and maybe give me a hand with the training?"

"Sure. Well, I'll give it a try anyway, and I can still blow hell out of a dog whistle. With a pointer pup that ought to come in handy." And they both laughed.

"Do any duck hunting?" Luke asked.

"Too much, probably," Jed said. "My wife said that if I had spent any more time sitting out in Jackson's Marsh the muskrats would have built their house around me."

"Retrievers?" Luke asked.

"Labs. Had some mighty good ones."

"That figures," Luke said. "After wrestling with those pointers you need a nice, soft, biddable dog. I'm a Chesapeake man, myself."

"You are?" Jed said with a grin. "You don't look too bit up."

Luke stopped his rocker in mid-rock and regarded Jed with complete disdain. Then he lifted a long, gnarled finger and pointed it at his adversary. "Jed Dawson," he said, "you've got an awful lot to learn about dogs." And just as he was about to launch into a spirited defense of the Chesapeake retriever, the porch lights signalled an end to the debate by blinking off and on.

The two old men got up slowly from their chairs, looked at each other for a minute, and then shook hands.

"Good night, Jed."

"Good night, Luke—and don't forget our date to train that pup."

"I won't," Luke said.

As he turned to leave he said, "See you tomorrow. There's a lot of things I've got to straighten you out on." Jed laughed and waved.

As Luke settled down on his narrow bed for the night, it somehow seemed softer. He stretched out his long, lean limbs, sighed, punched the pillow once, and with almost a smile on his lips went immediately to sleep. And off in the swamp the horned owl hooted again—five times.

2 WHERE DID YOU PUT YOUR HEAD?

EVERY family has its own private collection of stories, its own litany of anecdotes and incidents in the family history that are told again and again. Sometimes they are serious accounts. Sometimes they are not. Often they are not very important to anyone but the teller and are greeted with a fixed smile and a slightly glazed look in the eyes of the listener. As I recall, though, the lack of interest on the part of the audience seldom dampened the desire to tell the story again.

My grandfather Mitchell had a story, and although it was innocent enough, it never failed to stir up a gathering and fluster my proper grandmother. It all took place years ago in an upper Pullman berth on a night train crossing the plains of Nebraska. Grandad was on his way to a duck hunting camp on the Platte River and had asked the porter to call him in time to dress and get his gear together to drop off the train at a short whistlestop along the banks of the big river. Somehow, the porter forgot to shake Grandad awake until only a few minutes before the train came to a stop. Awakened from a deep sleep, Grandad thrashed around in the narrow confines of his upper berth, scrambling into his clothes. "To this day," he said, "I don't know how I did it, but I got into my long woolen underwear upside down with my arms through the legs and my legs through the arms. I thought it felt a little strange, but there was no time to change." Then he laughed and said, "I don't recommend the practice." There was always laughter, and then my grandmother, blushing like a schoolgirl, would say, "But, Charles, where did you put your head?"

Of all the voices from the past, the clearest is that of my dad saying: "Chappie and I were all ready with a big set of decoys early one morning on Pritchard's Point at Winneconne, and

5

here comes old Emil up the lake in his big red rowboat with an old double gun sticking up out of the stern. He kept on coming and rowed right through our bluebill decoys, tangling them up on both oars. We yelled and waved at him, and all he did was keep rowing and wiping the tangled lines off his oars and saying, 'Goot morning! Goot morning!' And then he disappeared around the point.

"We were out in the blocks in our skiffs trying to straighten them out when we saw a big bittern flapping slowly along over the point. We heard a shot, and the bird went down. Then we heard another shot, followed by Emil calling ''Elp! 'Elp!' So we went to his 'elp, and there he was, up to his neck in the marsh.

" 'Where's your boat?' we asked.

" 'I'm in it,' Emil said wide-eyed. 'That darn shidepoke flew over me, and I shoots him. He falls in da boat and goes to peck me, so I shoots him again and zunk da boat.'

" 'Serves you right, you old fool, for shooting everything that flies,' Chappie said.

"So," Dad said, "between our two skiffs we gradually eased Emil over to a muskrat house so he could climb up out of the water. Then we dug around, found his gun, floated his big, heavy capsized boat over to the edge, and pulled it up on the bog. All this time, Emil just sat there and watched us work.

"Finally he waded over, got his gun, and said, 'I guess I can't help you fellers any more, so I'd better go by home.' And off he went along the shore.

"Chappie looked at me and said quietly, 'If I thought I could reach him from here, I'd help him along with a load of sixes.' "

When it came to comparing the ballistic performance of various rifle calibers, and it often did, Dad had his story of Billy Robinson and the Englishman. It was during the logging days near the town of Amasa in the Upper Peninsula of Michigan. As Dad told it, "We were in a logging camp and met this Englishman who was cruising the area for white oak 'knees' used in the construction of English wooden sailing ships. He was a pleasant enough little guy, but somehow you got the impression that he found us, his American cousins, rather primitive and 'quaint,' if that's the word. He really annoyed Billy Robinson when he started carefully pointing out the superior features of his converted sporter, a .303 British rifle.

"Then he started on Billy's old Remington Model 8 in .35 caliber that he saw standing in the rack one night when we were all sitting around in the bunkhouse. Billy finally said, 'Well, the proof of any rifle is in the shooting, so I'll just bet you 10 dollars (which was a week's pay in those days) that the power of my old Model 8 will make your fancy rifle look like a peashooter.'

" 'You're on, my good man,' said the Englishman.

"The next morning was a Sunday and our day off, so after breakfast we all lined up at the woodpile behind the cook shanty to watch the contest. The rifle owners had agreed to put their money on comparative penetration, and the Englishman had the first shot. The target, the butt end of a pine log in the woodpile, was about 50 feet away. The .303 British bolt-action sporter cracked sharply, and the Englishman hit it square. The next shot was Billy's. He took a long time aiming that squat-looking old Model 8 autoloader but finally touched it off—and half the woodpile blew up with bark and wood flying in all directions. Nobody said a thing until the Englishman turned around to us in amazement and said, 'My word!' Billy was a good rifleman, but hitting that dynamite cap that he had put in the end of that log from 50 feet away took a lot of doing."

It was my Uncle Bill who made up the most elaborate stories, usually designed as a gentle rib of some pretention. His favorite target as a practical hunter was the so-called science of ballistics.

His favorite story was about deer hunting in Montana, and I can hear Uncle Bill say, "I jumped the biggest mule deer I ever saw at the foot of a big rock slide. He ran off about 50 yards and stopped behind a rock so that I could see only the tips of his horns. No way of getting a good shot unless I ricocheted my bullet off a big rock right alongside of him. As you know, I played a lot of three-cushion billiards in my youth, and I've always been a student of ballistics; so, I sat right down and started figuring out the exact angle of deflection needed to make a precise shot. First, I calculated the actual trajectory of my .30–06 220-gr. 'Core-Lokt' soft point bullet at that altitude, as well as its true muzzle velocity in my barrel length as opposed to the test barrel figures. Then, it was just a matter of barrel twist, the ballistic coefficient, and adding in the ogive and sectional density of the projectile . . . and I was ready to go. So I levelled my scope on the big rock—took a deep breath, let it half out—and squeezed the trigger."

Then he stopped until someone always asked, "Come on, Bill, what happened?"

"Something went wrong with my calculations."

"What?" they asked.

"I *missed* the blinking rock," he said.

7

GOODNIGHT, MRS. EVINRUDE 3

"THE way I heard it," said my Grandfather Mitchell, "was that my old friend Ole Evinrude was rocking peacefully on the front porch of his cottage on Pewaukee Lake taking it easy on a Sunday afternoon when his wife suddenly decided that she wanted an ice cream cone. The closest ice cream stand was about a mile and a half across the lake, and it was a hot August day. A long hard row in the sun, but Ole was a good husband. So he got up from his rocking chair, led the way down to the dock, helped Mrs. Evinrude and her parasol into the stern of the boat, and bent his back to the oars. There was not much talk between them until Ole stopped for a rest out there in the middle of the lake.

"His wife looked at him wiping his brow with the sleeve of his shirt and said, 'Ole, why don't you put a motor in this boat?'

" 'It's too small a boat to put a motor in!' Ole answered.

" 'Then why don't you put a motor on the *outside* of the boat?' Mrs. Evinrude asked.

"After a long pause Ole said softly, 'Why not?' "

And this, my fellow hunters and fishermen, was how it all began. Out there in the middle of a Wisconsin lake, sometime back in the '20s, in an old rowboat drifting quietly in the hot sun, an idea was born. It was a moment to which we could all well dedicate the blisters and backaches of a grateful nation who, now freed from the bondage of oars, take to the sea, lakes, streams and ponds in small boats and outboard motors. "Why not?" Ole Evinrude said, the rest is history.

Evidently, it wasn't long after Ole began to manufacture the first Evinrude outboard motors in Milwaukee when Granddad introduced this noisy but amazing invention to the quiet of Pine

Lake up in Forest County, Wisconsin. My grandparents had built the first cottage on this still-wild, beautiful lake years ago and spent each summer running a "resort"—as it was called. There were cottages to rent, but it was more of a fishing camp than a resort, I guess. No miniature golf and no juke boxes. I was lucky enough as a boy to spend many of my summers on Pine Lake. . . . guiding, selling minnows and renting boats as well as hunting, fishing and roaming the woods with my cousin, Red Cummings. What memories!

But back now to Granddad's new Evinrude outboard motor. It was a single-cylinder engine, sturdily built of solid brass and steel with a cast-iron cylinder. When we tried to pick it up, it seemed to weigh just a little short of a ton. You started it, occasionally, by spinning the horizontal flywheel with a fixed wooden knob. The starting cord came later. And when it was finally running, watch out for that knuckle-busting, hardwood knob whirring around in a deadly circle.

Contrasted with the steady, powerful hum of today's motors, this was an erratic, roaring monster that splashed water in all directions and threatened to loosen the nails and shake the very stern out of our heaviest rowboat. Unless you knew how to adjust the correct angle to trim the motor to the boat, all you got were foam and bubbles with very little forward motion.

In fact, on the very first day that Granddad tried it out—and went roaring and splashing down the lake—a little boy on the bank, curious at all the fuss, jumped into his rowboat and rowed right by Granddad as if to challenge him to a race. It was said that Granddad first muttered something about a "smart-aleck kid" but then laughed out loud at his own predicament and waved at the lad who was rowing furiously at least two full boat-lengths ahead of him.

Starting Granddad's new outboard motor was a constant challenge. After meticulously measuring the oil and gas combination and filtering it through a piece of chamois and a fine-screened funnel into the tank, you were ready. You opened the gas petcock of the built-in tank, adjusted the spark, grabbed the knob and rocked the flywheel a few times to prime the engine, and then gave it a hard spin . . . and another spin . . . and then a series of profanities and hard spins plus a few more half-hearted spins that completely flooded the engine. So then you turned off the gas and gave it another series of gradually diminishing spins until your wrist ached and you were exhausted. You then took the wrench and removed the single, gas-wet spark plug. First you blew on it with what was left of your breath and then you considered changing the spark gap. And if you did that, you ended up at the oars.

My grandfather had, however, developed a somewhat radical procedure for dealing with a flooded engine. After turning off the gas and removing the spark plug, he reached into one of his big hunting-coat pockets and drew out a wad of oakum. This was the tar-soaked hemp fiber we used for caulking boats.

Placing a wad of oakum in the spark plug hole, he would light the tarred fiber and then work the flywheel so that the compression of the cylinder would blow the yellow flames in and out of the cylinder, thereby "drying" it out. I doubt you will find this procedure approved by the U.S. Coast Guard. Occasionally there would be a small explosion in the cylinder that blew out pieces of the flaming oakum. Being a passenger in Granddad's boat during this operation called for constant alertness.

Since Granddad had the only motorboat on the lake, he often found himself and his boat at the head of a long line of row-boats filled with vacationing neighbors and their families headed for a Sunday picnic on the island. The picnic flotilla, usually organized by my grandmother, would form at Mitchell's Dock while everyone waited expectantly for a pleasant and effortless tow three miles down the lake to the island and back. With the boats all properly in line behind him, Granddad, as chief engineer and commodore, would turn to starting the engine. Sometimes it started with the first spin and cheers rose from the boats as tow lines tightened and we all moved slowly and happily down the lake. At other times there was a long and almost endless wait in the hot sun for Granddad to get the engine started while the homemade ice cream melted in the hand-crank freezer, the salad wilted, and the lemonade lost its chill. As Granddad struggled silently with the engine and the color of the back of his neck promised a major outburst, Grandmother from beneath her sun umbrella would say, "Now Charles, remember that it's Sunday and that there are children present. It will surely start—eventually." And as I remember, it always did—eventually—and away we went sailing along on a windless day without effort or the creak and grunt of oars.

And so she said to Ole, "Then why don't you put a motor on the outside of the boat?" So from all of us who love the outdoors and hunt and fish with a motor on the outside of our boats we say, "Goodnight, Mrs. Evinrude. Thanks and God bless you, wherever you are."

4 THE $10,000 BIRD DOG

SOMETIMES I find myself in a group of people staring silently at the everlasting TV with only a few mumbles to interrupt the hysterical screams of some poor, exploited lady on the quiz show who has just won a year's supply of cooking oil. I wonder whatever happened to the art of conversation. Whatever happened to story telling?

Maybe the energy crisis and a turned-down thermostat that tends to congregate people around a source of friendly heat may actually bring back a few fireside chats or restore a few hot-stove leagues. Maybe they will actually turn off the television and try talking to each other again.

I can't really remember the cat sleeping in the cracker barrel or the marathon checker games at the village store. But I can remember a potbellied stove in the back of the General Store in our town and the daily gathering in the winter of the town's male citizens who didn't seem to have much else to do at the time. It was sort of a club.

As I recall, the furnishings were sparse. A dog-eared copy or two of "Hunter, Trader, Trapper" magazine and last week's newspaper made up the library. The chairs were just plain chairs, made only to be sat on by the senior members. The younger set stood outside the circle or sat on the floor up against the wall. And the old stove on a cold, snowy day, breathed heat and quiet contentment on all who gathered about it. Through its door you could see the cheerful flames of the big white oak chunks giving back the sun of countless summers.

The conversations were many, and in this town the subject was often bird dogs and hunting. Herb Dixon, who was quite regular in his attendance, had spent most of his life as a professional bird dog trainer and field trial judge and had handled several national champions. Herb was well along in years, but when he started one of his bird dog stories, he straightened up in his chair like he was back in the saddle at the national championships at Grand Junction, Tennessee. His voice got firmer and there was fire in his eye. We young ones never knew quite how to take Herb Dixon's stories.

Some of them had to be true, especially when one of the older members would say, "That's right, Herb. I remember it well."

But we were never quite sure. Take the case of his story about the $10,000 bird dog. $10,000?

"That's right," Herb said. "The price was $10,000. When my boss, Mr. C. B. Calhoun first heard about it, he was certainly interested. Seems like he figured that any dog worth that much had to be a cinch to win the Grand National. And that's what Mr. C. B. Calhoun wanted to do. Man, did he want to do it. We had a kennel full of more pointers and setters than you could count. The feed bill alone would break every man in this room."

Herb looked over at me sitting on the floor up against the wall when he said this and I nodded wisely. My total cash resources at that time were about $2.62.

"Well," Herb continued, "soon as Mr. Calhoun traced down the rumor and the whereabouts of this high-priced dog, he called me in."

"Herb," he said "we've got to get that dog."

"Sure, Mr. Calhoun," I said. "It's your money, but how do we do it?"

"The owner lives pretty far back up in the Blue Ridge Mountains, but you can find him. Can you leave tomorrow?"

Well I worked for him and so off I went.

"Pretty far back in the Blue Ridge Mountains," Herb said. "I'll say it was. I got off the train at the end of the railroad and hired a rig that took me to the end of the road. Then I started to climb up the mountain following an old foot path that eventually led me to a clearing with a raggedy-looking corn field and a little cabin perched up there on the side of that mountain. And on the porch of the cabin was this old gentleman who stopped his chair in mid-rock, carefully got up, stared at me for a moment and then waved sort of shy-like.

"Good afternoon, sir," I said. "Are you the man who owns the $10,000 bird dog?"

"I am that man," he said.

12

"Well, I represent Mr. C. B. Calhoun, and he's interested in buying your dog."

"That's fine," he said. "Come on up and set awhile."

So we sat there for a while, looking out over the valley, and then the old man finally spoke up.

"I suppose for that kind of a price you'd like to see him run."

"Yes, I would like that," I said. "By the way, what's his name?"

"His name is Howard," he said.

"Howard? Isn't that an unusual name for a bird dog?" I said.

"Yes it is, but he's a very unusual bird dog," the old man answered.

"Is he around?" I asked.

"Yep, he's here all right. I'll go get the gun and we'll run him in the cornfield. There's a covery of quail that uses it pretty regular."

With that the old man went into the cabin and came out with a battered old double-gun and a handful of shells which he handed to me.

As I was putting the shells in my pocket the old man said softly, "Howard, let's go hunting."

Out from under the porch came the saddest-looking, beat-up, grey-muzzled old skinny setter I had ever seen. He shook himself a little and just stood there blinking in the sun.

"I was pretty set back by all this but didn't say a word as I followed the old man and Howard out into the cornfield."

"Hie on," the old man said, and Howard began to slowly putter around in the corn with only a few feeble wags of his motheaten tail to show he was hunting.

"Point," the old man called out.

And sure enough Howard had come to a halt that might have been a "point," but then he began to run in a big circle. Suddenly I realized that he was surrounding a covey of quail in ever-decreasing circles until he ran every last one of the birds down a gopher hole. With that Howard put his paw over the hole and looked back at me.

"What'll you have?" the old man said, looking me right in the eye. "Singles or doubles?"

5 MEET ANY INTERESTING DOGS LATELY?

'VE never made a survey, but I'll bet if you asked 100 people what really interests them, the honest answer would have to be other people. Even the dreariest TV talk show comes to life when the topic turns to other people. People are so incredibly varied that I can think of only one other animal that even approaches us. You guessed it. Dogs. Wouldn't it be an unusual switch if the host on that talk show suddenly turned to one of his guests and asked, "Have you met any interesting dogs lately?"

Although I never expect to have such an opportunity, my answer to a question like that would have to be, "Yes, I have. But every dog I ever met was interesting, and there are so many of them."

"Well," the host might say, "How about hunting dogs?"

"Now you're talking," I would say and immediately launch into a torrent of nonstop, disconnected anecdotes that would probably have the host signalling the control room to cut me off. But, on the other hand, I might just relight my pipe at the question and tell only one well chosen dog story.

I haven't smoked a pipe for years, but I might just plan to on this imaginary show. Pipe smoking gives you a calm, dignified and philosophical air. Have you ever noticed how a pipe smoker always seems thoughtful and introspective and speaks only a few wise words with calm deliberation. Over the years I have found that this is because if he talks too much his pipe goes out.

One of the things I enjoy about most hunting dog stories is the inability of the teller to stay anywhere near the truth, especially when the dog is his. For example, I was about to believe   15

Charlie Sage's story about the fastest foxhound in Tennessee. Charlie claims that this hound of his was so fast that it often ran ahead of the pack and ended up in front of the fox. That could probably happen, but when Charlie told me he had to teach that hound to run sideways in order to slow it down enough to keep in the pack, I began to doubt Charlie's veracity.

A story I might tell to confirm any question about Charlie Sage and the truth is his bragging about knowing a man in Gallatin who had the smartest foxhound in Tennessee. Charlie always seemed to stay within the state line in his claims. Maybe he figured it made his stories more believable. Charlie said he was right on the spot when they were running a fox back in the mountains with this unusual hound named Jed. They came to a deep chasm with a high cliff on each side.

"Darndest thing I ever saw," said Charlie. "Jed backed off to get a good run at it and then jumped, but halfway across the chasm he saw he couldn't make it so he turned around and came back."

It isn't very often that you hear the truth—and nothing but the truth—about a hunting dog. Aside from Charlie's stories, your best chance of getting a completely honest report on a dog's performance is to listen to what an unbiased participant says.

Just the other day I heard a true story about a Labrador retriever from the owner's hunting partner. It's a story that telling in public might possibly offend the proud owner so we'll dispense with names. The Lab in question is one of the best warm weather retriever trial performers I've ever seen. But last year, a few weeks before the duck season opened, the weather turned cold, and the water in our marsh was icy. On opening day the ducks flew well in the gray dawn, and the Lab's owner and his partner downed a pair of mallards on the first pass. Both birds fell well out in front of the blind in the tall grass. On the command "Fetch" the Lab charged down to the water's edge and stopped short.

"So help me," said the partner, "he put in his paw slowly like a toe in the bathtub and then quickly pulled it out. He whined a little and then came bouncing back to the blind and sat down. Then he looked up at us as if to say, 'Not this time, boys. It's too cold.' Well, we tried again and again to get him to go but he wouldn't budge. So we pulled up our boots and tackled the tall grass.

"Halfway out in the marsh, I looked back and there was that

Lab sitting in the comfortable blind with his ears all perked up, watching our every move. It was a long and muddy search, slogging around in that cold marsh, but we finally found both ducks. The dog welcomed us back with a lot of friendly tail-wagging and eagerly nosed the birds. I was about to forgive him a little when I suddenly saw that he had eaten our lunch. Not just a few bites. The entire lunch. He had neatly unwrapped all the sandwiches and they were gone. I searched frantically through the paper bags but couldn't even find my apple. He had eaten it. Completely. Didn't even leave me the core."

Further questioning revealed that since the hungry Lab couldn't figure out how to open the Thermos bottle, they still had hot coffee for lunch. We also heard later from the owner that the partner ate one of the Lab's dog biscuits. The partner vigorously denied this. "I only tasted it," he said.

On second thought this probably wouldn't be a proper story for a general TV audience. You'd have to be a crazy duck hunter to appreciate the full impact of such a sad but true tale. However, if you are a bird hunter you've probably already heard about the quail dog that never made a false point. (But once I get this pipe relit you'll find it hard to stop me.) The dog's owner, undoubtedly a cousin of Charlie Sage, told me the story the other day.

"From the time she was a little puppy and locked up on a robin in the backyard," he said, "that setter of mine never made a false point. If she pointed, you could bet your bottom dollar there was a bird there. One day, though, we were coming back to the car after a quail hunt, and I'll be darned if she didn't freeze solid on another hunter coming down the road.

" 'Howdy', I said. 'Judging by my dog, you've got some birds in your coat.'

" 'Nope,' he said. 'Just started.'

" 'Maybe then you've got a quail sandwich in your pocket?' I said.

" 'Nope. No lunch,' he said.

" 'Beats me,' I said. 'This is the first false point I ever saw her make. By the way, my name is Bill Sage, what's yours?'

" 'Bob White,' the man answered."

And I think my pipe just went out again.

EVERY DOG
NEEDS
A BOY 6

IT wasn't that Jimmy Bascom was really a bad kid. My wife said, "It's just that his parents have given him everything but time and attention." In a town as small as ours I'm afraid that Jimmy's problems were apparent to everyone. He seemed like a nice enough kid—not much for smiling, but with a shy "hello" for everyone.

But whenever there was trouble involving our young ones, you could rest assured that Jimmy was in the thick of it. Vandalism in the high school, driving without a license, drag racing on the new highway, and truancy all added up to a pretty sad record for Jimmy Bascom. He was only a high school freshman, but it looked as though Jimmy was on a path that could lead to serious trouble.

Our next door neighbor, Judge Weaver, had just retired from a distinguished career on the bench and was now working full time on his gun collection, hunting, fishing and gardening. One day we were talking over the back fence as Jiggs, his springer spaniel, and I watched the Judge weed his tomatoes. Jiggs followed the Judge everywhere and carefully inspected everything he did. I, too, was better at watching than weeding, but I finally said, "I see that Bill Bascom's lad, Jimmy, is in trouble again with the police."

"Too bad," the Judge said. "Looks like a classic example of delinquent parents. They don't seem to care what he does."

"Well, I don't know," I said. "I hear that Bill really laid it on him when he and Jan got home the last time and found out what Jimmy had done."

"Got home? Here they have a problem child and spend most of their time avoiding him. I wish I could spend some time with that boy."

18   "Think you could help him?" I asked.

THE BACK PAGE

"Look," the Judge said, straightening up from his weeding. "My business for years has been dealing with the problems of people and their relation to society. I could help him."

"Okay," I said. "It's not really my concern, but Bill and I are old friends so I'll tell him."

"Fine," the Judge said as he and Jiggs moved to the onions.

The next day I just happened to run into Bill Bascom in front of his office, loading his golf clubs into his car. We talked for a while and then I asked, "How's your golf game?"

"Awful," he said, "but it gives me a chance to get away."

"Does Jimmy ever play with you?" I asked.

Bill looked at me for a long moment and then he said, "He's not interested. A lot of my games involve customers. You know how it is."

"Does he hunt with you?" I persisted.

"No, not that either. He's crazy about dogs and guns, but I just haven't had the time," and his voice trailed off. "Isn't he pretty young—and unsettled—to handle a gun?"

"Age isn't the only measure," I said. "Why don't you send him over to see Judge Weaver and his guns?"

"Sounds good," Bill said with some relief. "I'll do that."

We were up at the lake for the summer, so I didn't get a chance to check on how the Judge and Jimmy were getting along or whether they had ever gotten together. One fall Saturday morning, however, I was glad to see Jimmy ride his bike up the Judge's driveway. Jiggs greeted him with his old tennis ball and dropped it at his feet with a loud bark and a lot of welcoming wiggles as only a spaniel can do. Jimmy patted Jiggs, sort of waved at me, and went into the house. Jiggs sat down with his tennis ball and waited for his friend.

That afternoon I saw the Judge in his garden and went out to watch him. After properly admiring his tomato crop, I asked, "How are you doing with Jimmy Bascom?"

The Judge sighed and said, "I wish I knew. He's a hard kid to figure out. Polite enough, but he just doesn't seem to trust adults. He never really smiles, and he's suspicious of everything I try to tell him. Still in trouble at school. My wife says I'm wasting my time. Maybe I am. The only one around here who seems to understand him is that crazy dog of mine. They're inseparable. Probably the only reason he keeps coming back."

"How did that happen," I asked.

"Hours of throwing that old tennis ball that Jiggs carries around. You know he won't retrieve for just anyone, but he runs himself ragged for Jimmy."

"How's the hunting been?" I asked.

"Not bad at all." The Judge brightened up. "Taking Jimmy on his first hunt next Saturday. How about joining us?"

"Thanks, I'd like to," I said. "Can Jimmy shoot?"

"You'll be surprised," the Judge said. "He's a natural. Can't fool him any longer with a hand trap."

Next Saturday came in shining. One of those rare autumn days when you feel good all over and happy to be hunting again. The three of us with Jiggs started out west of town and worked the first big cornfield without moving a cock pheasant, but two hens did explode right in front of Jiggs' eager nose. Jimmy snapped up his gun and then put it down slowly as the hens sailed away. "Boy! They really move, don't they?" he said.

I could see the mounting excitement in his face, but he handled his gun safely. And that was it for about the next two hours. Nary a bird in spite of a hard-hunting Jiggs. It was sad to see Jimmy's enthusiasm slowly dwindle. Then a cock pheasant went cackling out on the Judge's side, and he nailed it neatly. Jiggs was on the bird at the first bounce, and in spite of the Judge's whistle, he made a beautiful retrieve—to Jimmy.

"What shall I do?" said Jimmy.

"Take the bird, Jimmy. You carry him," the Judge said.

"No sooner had Jimmy pocketed the big bird when it was my turn as another rooster flushed in front of me and I got him. Again Jiggs made the retrieve to Jimmy. Sitting at his feet, bird in mouth, waiting for his hand.

And, then, as if it had all been planned, it was Jimmy's turn. A tough, towering shot, and he did it well. Jiggs scooped up that rooster on a dead run and headed for a widely smiling Jimmy, and if I ever saw a happy dog it was Jiggs. He wiggled all over and vigorously wagged what little tail he had. When Jimmy took the bird out of his mouth, Jiggs let out one joyous bark. As Jimmy leaned over to pat him, I thought I saw tears in his eyes. "Good shot," we both said. The Judge blew his nose hard twice and said, "Looks like we'll have to take you along on every hunt, Jimmy. You've got to handle Jiggs."

This was all a long time ago, and whether or not it had anything to do with a change in Jimmy's conduct I'll never know. But when we all attended Jimmy Bascom's high school graduation to hear his speech as the head of his class, Jiggs went with us in the back of the Judge's station wagon. And he took his old tennis ball along, too. Just in case.

20

7 PICK UP YOUR STOVE AND WALK

H E was known as "The Iron Man of the Hoh" and lived alone far up on the headwaters of the mighty Hoh River in the wilds of Washington's Olympic Peninsula. He was a cougar, bear and elk hunter and a veteran trapper. The tales of the strength of this solitary, wilderness man are legendary. Of all the stories about the Iron Man, the one I remember best concerns one of his semi-annual trips to the town of Forks to sell his furs and buy supplies.

Fur prices were up, and the Iron Man realized enough profit to buy a big, secondhand, cast iron kitchen stove to bake his sourdough bread and warm his log cabin. When the clerk in the general store talked about hiring a horse and wagon to haul the stove up the river road, the Iron Man said that wouldn't be necessary because he'd just carry it home along with his other supplies.

And so, with the help of the clerk, two bystanders and the proprietor, they got the stove up on his back, and he started for home. The story goes that all went well until about two or three hours later on the trail when he was surprised to find that he was getting a little tired. Finally, to his amazement, he actually had to put down the stove and rest.

"At first I thought I was getting sick," he said later. "Couldn't figure out what was wrong until I see that the dern clerk had put my 100-pound sack of flour in the oven." The Iron Man went on to explain that, "It wasn't the added weight of the flour that made the difference. It was that sack sliding around in the oven that kept throwing me and the stove off balance."

Ever since I was old enough to be fascinated by Sunday

school stories of Samson, the original strong man, I've been interested in tales of strength and endurance. Like many of us who have had a lifetime of hunting and fishing, I've seen a lot of strength and endurance in the out-of-doors. Have you ever noticed that unforgettable feats with pack and paddle or with tump strap and heavy loads do not always go with physical size? I once stood on the dock at the Eskimo town of Copper Mine in Canada's Northwest Territory and tried to lift one corner of a big bale of caribou hides that was sitting there—just to see what it weighed. I could barely budge that stack of hides, and while I was trying to figure out the total weight, a little square-built Eskimo came out on the dock, gave me a big smile, picked up the entire bale, and trotted off the dock with it. Talk about feeling puny . . . and I was almost twice his size.

I suppose that when your business is packing heavy loads on your back for pay you are bound to get pretty good at it. Nevertheless, I never fail to be impressed with the strength and skill of the professional bearer. Some of the best I ever saw were the skinny little Tamang porters in Nepal who carried our gear in the Himalayas. From the Trusuli River, up the old yak caravan trails to the Tibetan border and back, these tiny but tough and smiling little guys with their huge packs were amazing. My good friend and guide, Mahdukar Yaktimba, told us how our head porter, whose long Nepalese name had been shortened to LBJ, had won renown in the highest mountains in the world. On an expedition to Everest, they were crossing one of those nightmarish swinging bridges that spanned a deep and yawning chasm when one of LBJ's heavily laden porters from the lowlands decided that enough was enough and froze with fright in the middle of the crossing. There he hung like a motionless, fat spider in the thin web of the bridge. Whereupon LBJ, head porter, walked out on the thin slats of the bridge and spoke softly to the terrified porter until he slowly relaxed his white-knuckled grip on the ropes of the bridge. Continuing his quietly consoling words, LBJ picked up the porter and his pack and carried them *both* safely across the chasm. When the American trekkers complimented LBJ on his rescue of the porter, he said in Nepalese, "No other choice. He was carrying the food."

No matter how good your physical condition or how carefully you have trained for the rigors of a deer hunt, it's always a surprise to discover again just how heavy that medium-size buck can be when it's your turn to get him out of the woods. Although I have seen pictures of the mighty deer hunter, rifle in hand, with a big buck draped over his shoulders striding easily along the forest path, I have yet to see this in real life. I also have my doubts about those two smiling hunters strolling along through the woods with a nice fat deer strung neatly on a pole between them. Years ago on an early season hunt with no snow in the woods for an easy drag, my partner and I tried the pole-carry technique—once. I'm about six feet and my partner is about five foot, seven inches tall. Really not much difference in height until you get on opposite ends with about 165 pounds of deer swinging heavily in the middle of a springy pole. I was stumbling up and down over the uneven ground and staggering in and out of the brush and bull-briers with my shorter partner complaining loudly that he was carrying the full load. "If that's true," I puffed, "something sure as hell is sitting on my end of this pole." We finally got to laughing so hard that we dropped the whole load, untied the deer and dragged it the rest of the way to camp. As I remember, it was a long, long haul.

When it comes to the growing popularity of backpacking with all the modern, tubular pack rigs, freeze-dried foods, nested cooking utensils, nylon poptents, lightweight mattress pads and sleeping bags, I can only think of my old Trapper Nelson pack board with a rifle and ammo, a slab of bacon, a bag of flour, salt, pepper, one onion, a set of blackened tin cans, a skillet, a tarp, blanket roll, coffee, tea and a large can of bicarbonate of soda as an after-dinner surprise. And I remember how the straps of that old-fashioned pack seemed to be cutting permanent furrows in my shoulders while the dead weight of the load was slowly collapsing my arches.

Not long ago I met two young big game hunters who were doing it the hard way and packing back into the mountains on foot. I asked them if I could heft one of their fully packed modern rigs. "Go ahead," they said and helped me get into the straps. Man! All I can say is that if our young men can carry a pack like that, there isn't much reason to worry about the physical decline of our youth. With our current concern about physical fitness, jogging and even weightlifting, it seems that we can rest assured that the spirit of the "Iron Man of the Hoh" is still very much alive.

8 HOW TO REASON WITH YOUR BIRD DOG!

"I
F you plan to train a dog, you must first know more than the dog" is advice of long standing to all would-be dog trainers. While this admonition may seem to be only a flippant wisecrack, the truth of it often becomes painfully apparent as you open training negotiations with your first bird dog. The dog often does know a lot more than you do.

The cute puppy that kept you awake all night, chewed up the leg of your wife's prize chair and introduced some permanent new designs to the parlor rug has now become a dog. What's more, this dog has somehow managed to become a part of your life. Your attitude towards him or her is almost that of a proud, often exasperated and sometimes bewildered parent. But never underestimate "the child" because dogs are clearly altruistic. They have the power of loving something outside themselves.

If you have read this far in the fond hope that I am about to reveal some carefully kept secret of dog training that will solve all your problems, I wish to apologize. As far as I know there are no such instant solutions. In fact, I've been a sympathetic observer much more than a contestant on the often stormy field of "training your own bird dog."

Long ago, I was taught to shut up when the dog you're hunting with isn't yours. Conduct in the field is a matter between the owner and his dog and no matter how tempted you are to offer valuable advice—to both of them—it's bad manners to do so.

I once broke this rule. My good friend and hunting partner, 25

Alex Stott, is a very persuasive and articulate guy. Now retired, he once successfully directed thousands of people in his role as a corporate executive, and believe it or not, he has carried these powers of persuasive discussion into the field of dog training. He argues with his dogs. He tries to convince them with logic and friendly persuasion to recognize the errors of their ways and correct them.

That hunting day his discussion with his yellow Lab, sitting at his feet and looking up at him, so help me, went like this: "Now, Belle, I am truly disappointed in your performance. I need your cooperation. Only last Wednesday I distinctly told you to hunt closer. I thought we agreed on that, but now you've done it again by deliberately busting that cock pheasant way out in front of your friend, Jack, and me. Didn't she?" he said, turning to me.

"I think it was a running bird, but keep me out of this. I'm neutral," I replied.

Then I broke the rule. "Ye gods, Alex," I said in exasperation, "Wouldn't it be better to reprimand her with a hard slap of your cap and a loud 'no!' than just talking it over with her? You act like she understands you."

"Understand me? Of course she does. Didn't you see her nod her head?"

"If I did," I said, "it's about time for me to go back to the car and lie down."

The hunt continued in silence and Belle behaved perfectly. One of the best Labs I've ever seen, she now went about her business without a flaw. After a well-handled bird, a close flush and a perfect retrieve, I complimented Alex on his dog.

"Yes, she's working well now," Alex said with a big grin. "Good thing I had that discussion with her."

While I doubt that "discussion" as a training technique can be found in the usual dog training book, I once found a book that completely solved my problems with a new dog. The dog was Bones, a young Brittany spaniel that I had bought from Dr. Joseph P. Linduska at Remington Farms in Maryland.

Joe said, "He's got speed and a fine nose. Trained on quail, but he will make a good pheasant or grouse dog."

That was enough for me. Joe knew dogs and I knew Joe.

With great expectations, I opened the pheasant season with my brand new dog. I introduced Bones to my hunting companions with some pride as a Linduska-trained Brittany. Then I'm afraid I also said, "Just watch him go."

HOW TO REASON WITH YOUR BIRD DOG!

Well, for some reason or other he didn't "go" at all. Much to my chagrin and the ill-concealed amusement of my friends, he just wandered around in the woods and fields like a lost soul. Although he seemed to be enjoying the outing, he spent most of his time looking for me with an occasional sniff at some late fall wildflowers and a long, pensive gaze at a butterfly that suddenly flushed before him. My friends watched him "go" all right. They watched him go back to the car with me for a long, silent ride back home.

That night after dinner, my wife and I were sitting in front of the fireplace. Bones was stretched out on the hearth rug as though he were all tuckered out after a hard day's hunt. Some hunt, I thought. Looking for an answer to my problem, I was reading that great book "Training Your Own Bird Dog" written by the late Henry P. Davis. I had worked with Henry and knew his monumental "The Modern Dog Encyclopedia" as the ultimate authority.

My wife, Ruby, looked up from her paper and said "What are you reading?"

I held up the book and said, 'I'm reading Henry's description of what a good bird dog should do."

"Why don't you read it to Bones?" she said and went back to her crossword puzzle.

So I did just that. I read in a loud, clear voice what was expected of a good bird dog. As I started to read, Bones opened one yellow eye and seemed to be listening.

Now I know full well that Bones' initial performance was due entirely to his long trip from the Farms to a strange and new place with a new game bird and boss.

But I also want to report that on the next Saturday after our "fireside chat" Bones really did "go." He eventually became one of the best pointing dogs I ever owned. Obviously, that reading from the book had nothing to do with it. Obviously. But on the other hand . . .

NEVER SHAKE HANDS WITH A RATTLE-SNAKE

9

"THAT'S one nice thing about the fer-de-lance. He's one snake that hunts only at night so that if you happen to step on one early in the morning his venom is nearly all used up."

"Thanks a lot. That is very reassuring," I said and continued to watch intently each step as my guide and I made our way past the bases of huge jungle trees with their small animal burrows, the home of the fer-de-lance, on a trail in the mountains of Trinidad.

The fer-de-lance is a West Indian cousin of our rattlesnake. Up to seven feet long, he is deadly poisonous and has exceptionally long fangs but no rattles. So if there were any rattling noises to be heard as we walked along the trail it was probably my teeth knocking together.

It isn't that I am really afraid of poisonous snakes. Snakebite, after all, is way down the list of outdoor hazards as snakes rarely bite anyone. It's just that I don't want them to bite *me.* And so that morning I was glad to find that the fer-de-lances were all back in their burrows filling up their hypodermic fangs for the night shift as we walked quietly by their houses.

"Quechua" is a common language spoken by the natives of South America. To the foreigner it might as well be Klickitat or ancient Greek. And when it's delivered at high speed and mixed up with Spanish and much waving of the arms, you had better listen closely.

It all started when our guide, Jorge, asked one of the Yumbo Indians who were with us on the Napo River in Ecuador to take me back to a lake in the jungle where the piranhas live. Like most visitors to the Amazon area, I wanted to catch one of these ferocious little fish just to see what it was all about. The Indian was protesting vigorously and then I heard him say "sucuri"

28

and something that sounded like "serpiente gigantico" which added up in both Quechua and Spanish to that giant snake, the anaconda. Some weigh 250 pounds and are 35 feet long.

At this point I ended the discussion by also waving my arms and shouting calmly, "O.K., O.K. The deal is off."

In spite of the often lurid accounts we hear about poisonous snakes, did it ever occur to you how seldom the average outdoorsman actually encounters one? Raymond Ditmars, famous herpetologist (snake expert) who had collected and studied venomous reptiles all over the world, once said that a typical wooded area of the Catskill Mountains about 40 miles from New York City, with its population of rattlesnakes and copperheads, contained more poisonous snakes per square mile than any place in the world he had ever studied. So if you are really interested in poisonous snakes, you have to hunt for them. If you're not interested, just leave them alone, and they will usually treat you the same.

Common sense dictates, of course, that we should be constantly aware of where we are putting our hands and feet in snake country. And don't do what I did on the Y.O. Ranch in Texas a few years ago. During a lull in a deer and turkey hunt one day, an armadillo scurried across the trail and disappeared down his burrow. Always fascinated by these strange little armoured critters, I ran after him and then reached down the hole to try to catch him by the tail.

It was a deep hole, and when I was lying on my belly reaching down as far as I could, the Texan guide said quietly, "I wouldn't do that if I were you. There's likely to be a big old rattler living in that hole, too."

My reaction to his suggestion was so violent that I almost dislocated my shoulder pulling my arm out of that hole. Not only did this teach me a natural history lesson I've never forgotten, it also made the guide laugh until I thought he'd split a rib. But he wasn't just fooling me either. That's where the diamondback rattler often lives, so don't go sticking your arm down armadillo burrows. You may end up shaking hands with a rattlesnake.

If you are truly interested in avoiding rattlesnakes, here's another bit of advice. Don't try catching grasshoppers in the tall grass of a Montana meadow unless you look first before you grab. It was a long time ago in the valley of the beautiful Boulder River. My wife and I were collecting hoppers for trout bait along the edge of a field of timothy hay and alfalfa. We'd watch the hoppers flushing ahead of us and then look for the motion of the tall timothy stalks when they lit. We then grabbed down along the grass and caught the hopper. All went well until I misread a motion in the grass and almost grabbed the head of a big western diamondback rattlesnake. He was "in the blue" or shedding his skin and probably temporarily blind. He buzzed as he struck at my hand, and I swear I could hear his teeth click—but he missed me by an inch. My wife, who is a Montana girl with a great respect for rattlers, was right behind me, and although she still indignantly denies it, immediately established a new unofficial world record for the standing backward broadjump—all the way back to the road in one jump! Not to be outdone, I picked up a nine-foot, rough-hewn old wagon tongue made out of a heavy cottonwood log that was lying in the grass and tried to kill the rattlesnake. My adrenalin level must have been right up to the brim because Ruby said it looked as though I had uprooted a telephone pole and was swinging it down over my head like a broom stick. The last I saw of the rattler was his tail disappearing down a hole between two rocks.

After we calmed down a little I went fishing, and Ruby went back to the car. Later on in the day I picked my way carefully back to the same place to see if the rattler was there. He was nowhere in sight, but the nine-foot cottonwood wagon tongue was there, and it was so big and heavy that I could barely lift one end off the ground. That snake had changed me into Superman for one fleeting and unforgettable moment.

Evidently the horror tales we hear of snake pits covered with wall-to-wall crawling death just aren't so. Snakes are loners. A few years ago I was making a tour of the Arizona desert with some wildlife experts after the North American Wildlife Conference in Phoenix, and we suddenly walked into not one, but three, western diamondback rattlers. It was March, and they had evidently just come out of hibernation.

Steve Gallizioli, Chief of Research for the Arizona Fish and Game Department, with years of experience in the southwest, said, "That's the most rattlers I have ever seen in one place at one time."

They avoided us, and we avoided them. So don't be a trigger-happy snake hunter. If you meet a snake, poisonous or non-poisonous, just remember that he also has a place in the scheme of things. He's probably out hunting too. But not for you. Whenever you can, just leave them alone.

10 HOW TO USE CAVIAR TO STOP SMOKING

T
HERE comes a time in life when what you don't do becomes more important than what you do. I am at that stage now when I am constantly being told, "Don't smoke, don't overeat, don't get too tired, and don't forget to turn out the lights in the garage."

Take the matter of being told "don't smoke" with which I reluctantly agree. Today there are all sorts of methods designed to help you stop smoking. They range from hypnotism to inspirational group therapy meetings in the basement of a local church.

If you are really interested in how to stop smoking, as one hunter to another, I am about to describe one sure-fire procedure. To qualify for this treatment you must first be a duck hunter and be able to paddle a duck skiff for at least two miles into the teeth of a strong northwest wind.

It all happened years ago. It was early November, and my dad had gone back to Lake Winneconne, Wisconsin, to visit some old friends and go duck hunting. I was still in school at Madison, Wisconsin, but managed to meet him on that Friday night at the town center—the only bar in town.

Beer had just been legalized, and Spot's Place was filled with hunters, guides, commercial fishermen and lumberjacks. Dad hadn't been back to Winneconne in years, and soon an impromptu reunion party began to shape up.

The beer was still pretty new, but the food was unforgettable. Spot was an old hunting partner of dad's and kept remembering

31

something new to put up on the bar to go along with the beer. I can see him now coming out of the big walk-in cooler at the back of the place with his first offering. It was a covered dish of the local and properly ancient Limburger cheese. When the cover was removed it almost blew out all the lights in the saloon. Being both brave and hungry, I soon found out that the aromatic Limburger was delicious when thickly spread on a slice of German rye full of caraway seeds. Next was a big slab of smoked Winneconne Lake sturgeon which has to be one of the noblest of all smoked fishes. White, flakey and smokey, it went down well with the big schooners of beer and the pickled eggs.

Knee deep in "remember whens" and duck feathers of the past, the talk finally turned to the relative merits of caviar makers in the town. Winneconne was not only blessed with the lake sturgeon, some of which grew up to seven feet and weighed 200 pounds, but it also had several Russian-born immigrants in the town who knew the intricate secrets of preparing caviar from the roe of these big fish. Those who knew said it was equal to the famous Beluga caviar from the Caspian Sea which sells today for $200 per pound. As luck would have it, one of these Russians was in our group at the bar, so he went home and returned shortly with a big grin and a mason jar of his special caviar. We tried to pay him, but he refused and began to spread the thick, dark fish-egg jam on the rye bread and top it with a slice of Bermuda onion. So caviar was added to the menu—and more beer—and more caviar.

Fortunately, closing time came to our rescue, and Dad and I started down the deserted main street and over the long bridge across the Wolf River to the little old hotel on the bank of the river. The north wind was blowing hard enough to blow the ashes off my cigarette, and we could hear the waterfowl talking in the dark out on the big lake. I was young, and sleep came fast in the sagging hotel bed on what they used to call a "pick-handle" mattress.

The alarm clock shattered the dark, and I rolled out of my lumpy bed. I dressed hurriedly, came awake with a splash of cold water from the pitcher and bowl and went down to join Dad for breakfast. Somehow I wasn't feeling exactly fit or hungry, but I managed to put away a "short stack" of buttermilk pancakes with real maple syrup, several fried eggs swimming in grease and generous helpings of strong, garlic-cured bacon, a specialty of the house. With this and too many cups of ink-

HOW TO USE CAVIAR TO STOP SMOKING

black coffee, I began to feel a little better, but not much. The coffee tasted strangely of caviar.

In the light of a lantern on the hotel dock, we loaded up our Green Bay duck skiffs with decoys, shells, guns, lunches, push-poles and paddles. The wind had gone strong to the northwest, and we knew it would pick up even more at daybreak. Mickey Korn and Eddie Marine, local boys, joined us out of the dark in their skiffs, and we started up the river and into the big lake headed for Pritchards Point. When we pushed out from the lee of the dock and the wind hit us, I knew we were in for a long, hard two-mile paddle to the point. Mickey and Eddie, both powerful paddlers, were soon in the lead, and Dad and I trailed along behind.

It was beginning to show a little light in the east as we paddled up through the huge rafts of ducks that roared off the open water ahead of us. What a sound as thousands of canvas-backs, redheads, bluebills, widgeons and mallards took off and tens of thousands of coots galloped along the dark water before us.

The wind was now stiffening, and the paddle seemed heavier with every stroke. Icy, black water broke and curled over the bow and along the cowling, but I was still fairly dry in the cockpit of that good, little cedar skiff. Beginning to puff and feeling a little queasy, I was glad to see the high, yellow quill grass of Pritchards Point. I eventually made it to the point and, with one final push of the paddle, drove my skiff into the tall grass. My three companions were already setting out their decoys, but I needed a chance to catch my breath and calm my belly. Stretched out flat in the skiff, I watched the bluebills high overhead in the dawning light buzzing down the wind.

When Eddie Marine came back to the high grass I made my fatal mistake. Having discovered that my cigarettes were back at the hotel, I asked Eddie if I could borrow a smoke. Eddie fumbled around in his parka and came up with a bent pack of "Twenty Grands." At 10 cents a pack, they were a popular brand in the Depression, and I lit up. With one deep drag of that hard and acrid, caviar-tainted smoke I was promptly sick over the side of the skiff.

With the current cost of caviar, this is probably an expensive way to stop smoking, but I can assure you that was the last cigarette I smoked for many, many years. And as for caviar, the smallest bit on a cracker brings back the full taste of that "Twenty Grand."

11 SHANTY POETRY

THERE'S a shelf of old and battered duck decoys right over my desk, and about this time of year they seem to look down at me and come alive. Maybe it's the faint smell of fall that drifts in the open window, or the far-off call of Canada geese. Maybe these old blocks of weathered wood, shaped with long and careful cuts of bright cedar that curled against the sharp edge of a spoke shave, have somehow sensed that the ancient rites of migrating waterfowl have begun again. Or maybe it's just that I've been stuck in this office too long and should go out to the barn now and see if my duck boat needs a new coat of paint. If I should mention to my wife that my old decoys are coming to life, she will give me a long and thoughtful look and suggest that I take a nap. So I have said nothing about all this up to now.

It really began when I came across a small, red, leatherbound copy of *Long Shore* by Joel Barber. It was way in the back of the top drawer of my desk, and finding it at all is somewhat unusual. In fact, my wife claims that my rather loosely organized desk is a remote bit of The Bermuda Triangle and that any object placed on or in it will disappear without a trace, never to be seen again, which, of course, is a bit exaggerated. After all, I found this little Derrydale Press book given to me by Tom Marshall years ago. Tom was a friend of the author (I met him through Tom), and like Joel Barber, Tom also is recognized as an authority on decoys. If you're a decoy collector, you've probably seen Barber's book, *Wildfowl Decoys.* It was the first definitive work on the history of this ancient American craft and serves well as a delightful guide to the pleasures of collecting decoys.

Long Shore, however, deals mainly with gunning on the East-

35

THE BACK PAGE

ern Shore of Maryland, and it's written in "shanty poetry." Before any of you start backing off from the word "poetry," here is what the author says about it: ". . . things one hears in going to sea or coming ashore or sitting around, On the end of a wharf . . . but always kinda' private. Till you write it down on a piece of paper. Then according to me, it is . . . shanty poetry."

One of Joel's old decoys speaks up in a poem called "Americana." It goes like this: "Americana, the catalogue runs. And down below: Canvasback decoy from Maryland. And here am I on a museum shelf. Watching the dust rise and settle again. On faded curios. Americana: And I had rather lie at anchor off Havre de Grace. Or drift to leeward, derelict. And spend my days stored away on the Eastern Shore. In a shanty. Or on the bottom of the Chesapeake. That's where I would rather be. Waterlogged and bound in tendrils of wild celery." Shanty poetry.

No wonder these old decoys of mine seem to talk. And they are not all aristocrats either. Peeking out from behind a regal canvasback and an elegant redhead is the ivory-white bill of a lowly mud hen decoy. Properly called American coot, this black-feathered, three-toed noisemaker is not really a duck. It's a member of the rail family and related to the gallinules. I can remember when every good set of 40 to 50 canvasback and redhead decoys back in Wisconsin had at least five or six mud hen decoys added to the flotilla. Confidence decoys they were called. Like gull decoys, these mud hen blocks bobbing around in the set were designed to say "all is well" to passing ducks inclined to doubt the veracity of your decoys.

I just reached up and took down this coot decoy. It's solidly built of heavy pine and was made by George Sauerbreit—no doubt a solid man in his own right—who used it on Lake Puckaway near Princeton, Wisconsin, about 1925. George knew his mud hens, and he hasn't forgotten the red forehead shield or the narrow white border on the rear of the wing. Bill Johnson, my good friend, gave me this decoy, and according to his label the maker "was a lock tender on the Fox River, west of Princeton and a great hunter." (It would have been hard to find a waterman in those days who wasn't a great hunter.) "Crazy as a coot" is an old phrase and probably stems from the unusual vocal range of this ungainly, chicken-like "galloping duck." As I hold this decoy in my hand, I can hear all those strange sounds out in the marsh accompanied by a lot of splashing and fussing.

36

"Crazy" is right, and coot calls are variously described as croaks, toots, grunts, cackles, coughs, quacks, coos, whistles, squawks, chuckles, clucks, wails, and froglike plunks and grating sounds. Ye gods! What sounds! I'd better put him back on the shelf before he wakes up the cat sleeping in the sun on the window sill.

Looking down at me with almost a lifelike glint in his red, glass eye is a magnificent drake canvasback decoy carved by Bill Johnson out in Scandinavia, Wisconsin. "Bull cans" we called them . . . and with their thick red necks and full black breasts cutting the waves like a ship's prow, they fit the name. Right now I'd like to put him back on Blue Dog Lake in South Dakota . . . one of a big raft of decoys off the point at Hemingways. Let the wind go northwest and blow strong and steady down from the lonely prairies of Saskatchewan and across the flats of the Dakotas heading straight for the big, reed-filled marshes and lakes of Day County. Let them come by the thousands again, the legions of canvasbacks, redheads, gadwalls, bluebills, and sprig—waves of them across a darkening sky with the sting of snow in the air rattling against the hood of my parka. The call from my brother Bob is "mark right," and I'm about to make a perfect double when my wife calls out, "I thought you were going to rake the leaves today."

Sensibly postponing the leaves until the wind dies down, I pick up the little red book again and read about the old house Joel Barber bought on the Eastern Shore. "It's winter now and cold winds cry in the eaves of my old house. But fires burn in the old place. And wood-smoke drifts again, along the creek and over the river. And over a fire of white oak, breast down in a shining range, prime canvasback are roasting now."

The little book does it again, and in my mind's eye I am sticking my head into Mrs. North's kitchen in the old South Dakota clubhouse on Lake Minnewasta. She has just taken the lid off a huge, black roaster of fat canvasbacks. One to a person. And now she is carefully pouring a mixture of wild grape jelly and duck juice over the glistening brown breasts of the ducks.

The aroma is too much for me, and I say in trembling tones, "When do we eat?"

"Not until it's ready. And my woodbox is empty again."

And when I go out to the woodpile, the last rays of the setting sun light up a flight of bluebills whistling over the Pass. I can't tell it as well as Joel Barber does . . . but that was shanty poetry to me.

WHERE IS EVERYBODY? 12

COME on in, Alex. Let's go sit in the kitchen. Coffee's ready, so help yourself. Here's the morning paper. Not much good news in it, except for an editorial on the establishment of wilderness areas—and how much we need them in times like these. Makes sense, too. Looks like we are sort of apologizing for what we've done to the rest of the country. Wasn't it Mark Twain who said that man was the only animal that blushes . . . or needs to?

I guess all of us have to share in the blame, and the blushes too, when we take a hard look at what we've done to the land under the notion that expansion is always good and that bigger is better. We've made an ugly, concrete wasteland with foul rivers and garbage dumps where woodcock coverts used to be. Okay, okay, I know you've heard all this before. Just one more point, and then you can complain, too. It's just this. Why in the world can the backpacker, the camper and the fisherman feel free to roam so many of these wilderness places and yet the hunter is often banned? Don't people realize that if it weren't for the hunter there wouldn't be any wildlife to worry about?

But it does give me a pleasant feeling to know about the growth of wilderness areas. I guess you could be a barber in Bangor, Maine, or an insurance agent in Des Moines, Iowa, and you'd still feel good about knowing that somewhere there was an untouched and primitive wilderness in our country, and that someday you were going to take the wife and kids to see it.

Speaking of wives, did I ever tell you about the time Ruby and I were travelling in the Quetico-Superior canoe wilderness? We had just finished a long portage from Wolf Lake to the foot of Knife Lake. It was just before sundown, and not even a breeze ruffled the calm expanse of the long, narrow, blue lake stretching endlessly off to the north. As we quietly launched our canoe on the still lake, the silence and loneliness of the scene, so affected my wife that she turned around from her bow seat in the canoe and whispered "Where is everybody?"

I guess that's the true essence of wilderness. It's being where everybody isn't. It's being where you begin to feel what a small part you really play in the immense natural scheme of things. It diminishes you, and yet you feel a satisfying part of it all.

We've seen a lot of changes, Alex, you and I, in a lifetime of hunting and fishing around this country. The good old days for us, and yet when we were young we always heard from our elders about *their* good old days and how things would never be the same. I'll never forget what a feeling of wild and trackless prairie I used to get when my Dad told his story about riding across the plains of eastern Montana on a horse-drawn buckboard with a rag tied around the spokes so they could count the turns of the wheel and estimate their mileage. It was in 1910, and he was a young member of an advanced survey crew that was laying out a new route for the Chicago, Milwaukee and St. Paul railroad from Mobridge, South Dakota, to Miles City, Montana. He used to tell a story about two elk poachers who rode into camp one night. They had been hunting down in Yellowstone country, and all they had to show for their hunt were two bags of elk teeth. The two incisor teeth from each elk brought a good price, and the rest of the carcass was left to the wolves and ravens.

We've come a long way since then, and thanks to good management and law enforcement, the elk—as you well know—is now doing well all over the West.

It took a certain breed of durable and dedicated hunters to get along in the old days when the land was still wild. I wonder what my granddad would say today if he could take a hunting trip back to the prairie in a modern recreational camping vehicle. I remember his stories about farm wagons, cold meals— they had no wood to build a fire—and sleeping in the hay stacks out in the open every night. The height of luxury was a collapsible little tin stove that burned twists of hay to heat the coffee. I wonder what he would say about stereo, clean sheets, instant coffee and an ice cube maker in the Sandhills of Nebraska?

But there were compensations for the rigors of those early hunting camps. On granddad's first duck and goose hunting trip to the Platte River back in the '90s, both he and his companions spent their first night on the bank of the big river virtually without sleep. Not because of opening day jitters, but because of the almost deafening clamor of untold thousands of waterfowl moving about on the water all through the night. What an opening day that must have been!

Although I know that the developer is always accused of profiteering every time he moves against the wild land, I'm not quite sure what's wrong with making a profit. It's the basis of our whole system. What we need to do is to protect so firmly what's left of our wild land that the developer can't see a way to wiggle in and make a profit. With him it will be no profit, no deal. With all the talk about oil profits and the role that energy is playing in the balance of wilderness versus an eventual power black-out, I'm reminded of the story about the old settler who was "batching it" as they called it, on a run-down, little farm in southern Illinois. Barely able to scratch out a living, he was a little more than surprised when they made a big oil strike right smack in the middle of his farm. A local newspaper reporter went to call on him, and there he was, rocking and spitting over the front porch rail of his little shack with the big oil rigs all around him.

"Tell me, John," the reporter asked, "what are you going to do with all of your money?"

"Well," he said, "I don't rightly know, but I can tell you one thing. I ain't goin' to whittle out no more axe handles. When I need a new one, I'm just goin' to town and buy one."

There's a whole lot of wilderness areas I have yet to see. But I'm working on it. I just got back from a houseboat trip out in the back reaches of the Florida Everglades wilderness. Took a few pictures. Alligators, mangrove swamps, flight of ibis across the full moon and some interesting shots of the motels we stayed in. Only about 500 or so slides, so why don't you and your wife come over tonight. Oops, you choked on your coffee. You say you're going to be busy? Well, maybe some other time.

13 MY COUSIN AND THE GRIZZLY BEAR

"A bear suddenly raised up about 20 feet from me in the half-dark. I thought it was a black bear, so I yelled as loud as I could to drive it off. But it wasn't a black bear. It was a big grizzly, and he was on me in two jumps—all teeth and claws. I had just crossed a little creek that ran into the Yellowstone River, on the top of a big dead and down tree, and was making my way through the branches when he hit me. I swung at him with my fly rod as he knocked me down through the dead branches. My fall broke off a branch, and somehow I came up swinging it as a club. While I was walloping the bear, he was clawing my left shoulder and biting my middle. It was the nine aluminum fly boxes in my fishing jacket that probably saved my life. Together with my beating at him with that club and his biting the metal boxes, he finally decided he couldn't eat me and he took off running. I was sure glad to see him go."

"How many times did you swing that club at him?" I asked.

My cousin, Gordon "Red" Cummings, looked up at the palm trees in his Florida back yard for a moment and then he said, "Plenty. It's still all kind of hazy, but we evidently had quite a tussle."

"How did you get out of there after the grizzly left you?" I asked.

"Well, he had bitten through my right hand when I tried to hit him with my fly rod. It wasn't much of a weapon." Red laughed a little. "He'd clawed me up pretty good on my upper left arm and put six deep claw marks on my back. I was a mess, all right. Torn up and bleeding. I remember getting on my feet and picking up another club, just in case he came back. Then I wobbled up the hill about a quarter of a mile to my car. Had a little trouble with the ignition key and my chewed up hand, 41 but I made it back about two miles to our house at Mammoth Hot Springs."

Gordon's wife, Marlitta, who had been listening to Red's story, interrupted and said, "Now, Gordon, before you tell everyone about the reception I gave you at home, it's my turn. You have to remember that all this happened quite a while ago, July 7, 1953, to be exact. But it's still very vivid to me. We had just moved into a new U.S. Park Service job at Yellowstone with Gordon as an assistant engineer. I had finally completed the moving-in process, and the house was spick and span. Gordon had gone trout fishing after supper. Our daughter, Mary Carol, was only a little tyke then, and I had just put her to bed. Well, I heard the car drive up and Gordon coming up on the front porch. I looked out through the glass in the front door and in the dim porch light I could see he was all bloody. 'Gordon,' I said, 'if you've been cleaning fish again you can just go around to the *back door!*' And with that he lurched up against the door and fell into the living room right at my feet.

"It's funny now, about my trying to send him to the back door. People know I'm a proper housekeeper, and I've been kidded about it unmercifully. But it wasn't funny then. I immediately phoned the Government Hospital which, fortunately, was only about a mile and a half away. Then somehow I got Gordon to his feet and out into the car, but I couldn't get that old car into reverse to back out of the drive. Somehow I finally wrestled it into gear and away we went. The hospital people were great. It was 9:30 then, and Gordon was in surgery until 1:30. We were brand new in the park, and I was so scared and worried. Then a very nice thing happened. Another new park engineer named Melvin Thuring heard about Gordon and came to the hospital to sit with me. I'll never forget him or my good neighbor who came right over to stay with our little girl. Isn't it good to know how nice people can be when you need them? Gordon was in the hospital for nine days and then spent another 11 days there when he had a severe reaction to all those penicillin shots. Bear bites and claws are septic."

"Red, how do you feel these days about TV stories like *Gentle Ben* with the little boy and his giant pet black bear. Or how about Grizzly Adams frolicking with all of his bears in a field of mountain daisies?" I asked.

"Well, I hope that someone makes it clear to people and their kids that these are only contrived fairy tales and that a bear— wild or tame—is still an unpredictable and dangerous animal."

MY COUSIN AND THE GRIZZLY BEAR

"Did you ever figure out why that grizzly attacked you?" I asked.

"Probably startled him—and he sure as the devil startled me. Don't really know, but the doctor who took care of me said I was in a bad place. That's a grizzly run where the bears come down from the mountain and cross the river on their way to the garbage dump."

"Had there been any bear attacks before yours?" I asked.

"No. Statistically, up to that time, with one exception, mine was a *rare* example of unprevoked attack. It wasn't really much comfort," Red answered with a grin.

"What was the exception?" I asked.

"It happened down at the South Entrance. A Ranger's wife was hanging up clothes in the back yard with her two-year-old son close by. A black bear came into the yard and snatched her little boy by his head and carried him off. The mother's screams evidently caused the bear to drop the child from his jaws, and the bear ran off. The little boy recovered from the tooth punctures in his skull—but I'll bet that *Gentle Ben* isn't his favorite TV program."

"Did you ever go back to where you met the grizzly?" I asked.

"I did, and I found the club and what was left of my fly rod. Want to see them? I've still got my fishing jacket, too. It needs a little mending."

Red went back into their cool Florida house and came out with the club, several chewed-up short pieces of what had once been a fly rod, together with a blood-stained, tattered fishing jacket.

I studied the sturdy three-and-a-half-foot club about the size of a baseball bat and noticed that there was dried blood on both ends of the stick.

"Whose blood is this?" I asked.

Red took the club, and his hands tightened on the dry, hard wood.

"It's on both ends, so I guess some of it is mine, and some of it came from the bear."

Red stood there with the club, the pieces of the fly rod, and the torn jacket while I took his picture. Marlitta watched him proudly, and I might even have seen a small tear glisten behind her glasses. Red is retired now. His famous red hair is getting a little gray, and he has grown a little thick around the middle. But I can tell you this. If he ever has to go through another encounter with a grizzly, I still wouldn't bet on the bear.

14 WHICH GAME BIRD IS THE HARDEST TO HIT?

"WHICH game bird is the hardest to hit?" This is a question absolutely guaranteed to stir up any gathering of hot-stove-league shotgunners. Eyes light up and chairs are hitched closer to the circle as each member waits to tell his story of exactly how that big cock grouse just folded his wings and slid over the edge of the hill, never to be seen again.

Or maybe it's that stormy day your hunting partner came out to the duck blind after you had just scored exactly "zero" on three consecutive down-wind flights of canvasbacks.

"What loads are you shooting?" he asks.

"High base sixes," you answer. "Why?"

Then he says, "Well, with the results you're getting I thought you were shooting mashed potatoes!"

Very funny!

Another hard-to-hit duck story that I've heard is about the totally frustrated hunter who emptied his gun at a big flock of green-winged teal that buzzed his decoys and never touched a feather. So he stood up, shook his fist at the fast departing flock and cried, "Go, you little so-and-sos. If the world is round you'll be back in ten minutes!"

There is always something funny about an experienced but perplexed hunter who has consistently failed to connect . . . especially when it isn't you. I know it's not polite to laugh, but just thinking about the day my partner left the duck blind during a lull to hunt some jacksnipes that were sailing around the marsh still makes me chuckle.

45

"It won't take long, and I'll just get a half-dozen or so for lunch. They're delicious," Bill said.

"How about your gun?" I asked. "Full choked 32 inch barrel and duck loads? Not much of a snipe combination."

He looked at me with kindly pity and said, "You just let 'em get out a ways. After they straighten out and settle down you nail 'em."

Bill was an excellent shot, so I believed him and started to think about those fat, delicious little jacksnipies sizzling in the pan . . . not too well done. The lull in the duck flight continued, but I could hear Bill banging away back on the marsh. Finally he showed up. He just stood there and glowered at me.

"Well," he said, "why don't you ask me how I did?"

"O.K.," I said, "How did you do?"

"Not that it's any of your business, but I ran out of shells."

"How many did you get?" I asked.

"None! They never straightened out, and they never settled down," he said in a tone that dared me to continue the discussion.

He got back in the blind, and we just sat there without a word until the ducks started to move again. Bill missed two easy shots.

"What's the matter?" I asked.

He finally grinned a little and looking straight ahead said, "I think I bent my barrel on those delicious jacksnipes."

Then he looked at me and we both laughed . . . loud and long. Bill was a good partner.

When it comes my turn around the stove to vote for the hardest-to-hit game bird, I'm afraid I'll have to vote for the band-tailed pigeon. These tough, wild birds that fly the big forests of the West often seem to handcuff me when it comes to pointing a gun. I first met them on Whidbey Island in Washington during World War II. Yes, I said "Two," not "One." After all, it was only about 36 years ago. I was attached to the Naval Air Station Free Gunnery Training Unit at Whidbey, and George Selkirk was a shipmate. You Yankee fans must remember "Twinkle-toes" Selkirk. George relieved Babe Ruth way back when, and the same sharp eye that won him a spot on the Yankees for 17 years served him well as a gunner. He was a fierce man with a .50 caliber machine gun, as well as a very nice guy. Every once in a while our liberty from the machine gun range coincided, and we went hunting together. A busman's holiday. Training applicants for Naval Air Gunners Wings was a hot, full-time, ear-splitting job on a roaring machine gun range. We taught them to defend their bomber by learning to "lead, swing and follow through along the line of apparent motion" and knock attacking enemy fighters out of the sky. Our homemade maxim was, "To hit a moving target and put it out of *biz* . . . aim where it's gonna be and never where it *is.*" Bum poetry but it worked.

So by living and teaching these fundamentals of good gunnery every day, how could we ever miss an easy target like the band-tailed pigeons we had seen on our way to the range. No way. But pride goeth before a fall. As George and I started to stalk these wary birds perched high in a towering snag, their necks got longer and longer and finally, with a loud "clack" of their powerful wings, they catapulted out of the top of the tall dead trees. To me their "apparent motion" was unbelievably fast and only occasionally—very occasionally—did our shot charge put them out of "biz." In fact, we often seemed to shoot where they had been and seldom where they "is."

On our way back to the jeep, with only a few birds in hand, George shook his head and said, "If those pigeons had been Japanese Zeros I think we would have been shot down several times today."

I agreed.

According to Dick Baldwin, reputed to be one of the best grouse shots in all of New England, the "bird-out-of-a-tree" shot—like our band-tailed pigeons—is always a tough one.

Dick says, "When I was 13 years old the first grouse I ever hit came right out of Fuzzy Keeler's apple tree, and I haven't hit a bird coming out of a tree since."

The next year Dick, as a youngster, won the North American Sub-junior Trapshooting Championship and has been winning national trapshooting titles ever since, including being picked 14 times on the All American Professional Trapshooting Team. Therefore, Dick's vote for the ruffed grouse as the toughest game bird to hit bears considerable weight.

As you can readily see this casual research on the toughest game bird to hit has only begun, and we have yet to hear from the dove, goose and woodcock hunters, not to mention those hardy sidehill chukar chasers in Idaho. But I'm out of space and will have to close with a sign that I still remember as a kid at our local sporting goods store. It read, "To hit is history. To miss is mystery." Any votes out there on your toughest bird?

THE GREAT WATER FIGHT 15

DID you know that the latest scientific estimate of the amount of water on the earth is about 140,000,000,000,000,000 tons? You did? Well then, did you know that water covers three-fourths of the earth's surface? Or that the bodies of the four billion or more human beings walking around on the remaining dry one-fourth of the world are composed of two-thirds water? How about that? The immensity of such numbers concerning this wide and watery world make any comments I have on keeping this water out of my boots, sleeping bag, tent and boat seem trivial and self-centered. On the other hand, I seem to deal in such trivia, so here goes.

My first encounter with the menace of dislocated water was at an early age. I was just a little guy, and we were camped along the Pine River in northern Wisconsin. It rained. Man, how it rained! It was too wet to fish and too hard to keep a fire going, so we went to bed right after supper. The smallest member of the party, I was jammed up in the corner of our crowded tent with my head only a foot or so below the taut, wet, brown canvas roof.

"Whatever you do up there, kid, don't touch the canvas or it will leak" was the warning. "Watch out, boy. Don't touch that canvas."

Well, if you have ever yielded to the temptation of a "Wet Paint" sign, you know what finally happened. I touched it only once with an inquisitive finger, just a light touch on a spot right over my head. They were right. The spot leaked. All night. Drop after drop. Regularly and relentlessly on my head. Talk about Chinese water torture. I was too ashamed to complain or try to wiggle away, so I pulled the blanket up over my face and let it drip. I must have finally gone to sleep. But to this day, a dripping faucet on a rainy night keeps me staring wide awake, and I'm back in that tent in the rain up on the Pine River.

With all the numbers available about water I'm surprised that some out-of-work statistician hasn't figured out how much water leaks into hunters' and fishermens' boots each year. In my case it would have to end up in gallons. Not that I don't fight back with patches, tape and cement. It's just that I have never seemed to get the knack of permanently repairing a leaky boot or a pair of waders. I have, however, developed some techniques in the field of leak location and detection that have drawn considerable acclaim from the wearers of so-called "waterproof" footgear. In fact, I have thought seriously of entering this field as a consultant.

One of my most amazing innovations is "The Bathtub Test," in which you fill up the bathtub, put on the leaky waders, step into the tub and sit down carefully. In no time at all, you will feel the leak, whereupon you get out of the tub, remove the waders, and locate the leak.

In all fairness, though, I should tell you that my duck-hunting neighbor ran into some minor marital difficulties with this particular test. Following my instructions, he had just settled into the brimming tub wearing his chest-high waders when his eight-year-old daughter appeared wide-eyed at the bathroom door and then ran down the stairs screaming "Mama, Daddy's in the bath tub with all of his clothes on!" When his wife came running frantically into the bathroom, he tried to get up to explain what he was doing and slipped back into the tub with a splash that flooded the floor. In spite of his attempts at explaining the test, he was unable to calm his wife for some time. He finally gave up the test completely and bought himself a new pair of waders. The last time I saw him I thought he mumbled something about sending me the bill, but I didn't really hear him clearly.

Another major contribution that I have made to wader care and maintenance is "The Closet Test." When searching for an elusive wader leak, you need only a flashlight and a dark closet. Turn the waders upside down over your head, step into the dark closet with a lighted flashlight and close the door. With your head in the waders, you can easily locate the holes by running the flashlight over the outside of the waders and marking the leaks for repair.

Before carrying out this test, however, be sure to tell your wife what you are doing. A friend of mine neglected to do this, and when his wife heard strange noises in the closet, she threw open the door to be confronted suddenly with a strange apparition. Instead of fainting, she walloped him twice with a broom before he could identify himself with his muffled outcries.

"Once I got the waders off my head, she hit me again for frightening her," he complained.

Somehow he didn't think it was quite as funny as I did.

Working in the field of leaky boots research, it is sometimes necessary to abandon a proven technique in spite of its apparent value. One of the tests I no longer use or recommend is "The Clothes Line Test." In this test you merely hang your waders or boots on the clothes line and fill them up with the garden hose. Then you check carefully for leaks, mark their location, and dump out the water. In three or four days your boots or waders will be dry enough to patch and wear. A simple and direct test. But with the advent of gas and electric clothes driers, it has become increasingly difficult to locate a clothes line or even a place to hang one. Back yards now have become "family recreation centers" full of patios, plastic pools, barbeque pits, wrought-iron furniture and portable bars. You can't hang up your boots on a gas grill.

Another reason for dropping "The Clothes Line Test" from my recommended list was the regrettable fall day I hung up my leaky duck-hunting boots alongside my wife's freshly laundered bed sheets flapping in the sun and the breeze. (Does anyone remember how good those sheets smelled?) Well, as luck would have it, and through no fault of my own, the line snapped as I was filling up my boots with the hose, and down went the clean sheets on the muddy ground, accompanied by screams from the back porch. Even to this day Ruby warns me "not to hang those muddy boots on my clothes line." When I remind her that we no longer have a clothes line she says, "I don't care. Just don't do it." And I haven't.

I suspect that the fiberglass plastic boat was invented when someone sitting in a plastic bath tub (without his waders) suddenly realized that if the tub could keep water *in,* it could also be used to keep water *out.* So he got out of the tub, put on his pants, and invented the fiberglass boat. And for that I certainly thank him. No more struggles with wood versus water. No more cases like Ray Baldwin's wooden car-top duck boat that filled up with rain one stormy night. "Don't worry," Ray said, "it will leak out." And it did. No more of that with bone-dry plastic boats. So, take heart, hunters and fisherman. We may yet win the battle against out-of-place water.

16 STOP THE RIVER, I WANT TO GET OFF

WON'T you agree that most of life's real adventures are totally unplanned? They just seem to happen. Hardly any of us slam down the garage door and leave the house some morning grimly determined to go out and have an "adventure." An adventure usually turns out to be the result of a mistake we have made. And that's what happened to me when I decided that I was not yet too old to run a big white-water river. That feeling of power and speed as the deep, smooth lip of the rapids first seizes your canoe and then the challenge of a fast, rock-strewn, white water run is hard to forget.

The more I thought about it the more expert I became. Somehow I overlooked the day I came flying down the Deerskin River with a nice, fat buck in the bow of my Grumman canoe and was so impressed with my role as a fearless river runner and rifleman that I ran slam-bang into the only big rock in the rapids. I seemed to have forgotten that sudden cold bath and the sadly dented canoe. What I had my armchair imagination aimed at now was the mighty Colorado River and its tumultuous course through the Grand Canyon. Little did I realize that moving from the Deerskin to the Colorado was like going direct from the Little League to the World Series.

No doubt, many of you have seen the Grand Canyon so I won't try to describe it. That's what everybody says because it's indescribable, and then they go ahead and try to describe it anyway. One of the best attempts at a description of this magnificent hole in the ground was made by the old mountain man who was hunting and exploring in the area when he and his partner suddenly came to the rim of the Grand Canyon.

51

They both stood in complete awe and silence until the old hunter quietly said, "I don't know what it was, but something sure as hell has happened here."

Running the Colorado is no longer an exclusive privilege these days; thousands of people have done it. So why shouldn't my family and I give it a try? Pictures of the big rubber rafts riding serenely through the canyon with 15 or more happy passengers waving merrily at the camera were reassuring. With huge sausage-like pontoons, these 35-foot rafts were called "baloney boats" by the river man, and they looked fine to me. When my research revealed an old *Life* magazine picture of one of these big rafts in the process of upending in a huge rapid called Lava Falls, I was told that this rarely occurred. (Probably just what they told the passengers on the *Titanic* or the people living near Mount St. Helens.)

Since I wasn't quite sure what kind of boat we had signed on, I began to worry. Given a choice, I would have picked the *Queen Mary* and the spine-tingling thrills of shuffleboard on a calm day, but if pressed I would settle for one of those "baloney boats." Such details were of little concern to my wife strangely enough, since she is more of a strong wader than swimmer. There are very few swimming holes in her native Montana.

Nevertheless, both she and my daughter, Susan, who had enthusiastically agreed to join us said, "Why worry? These are experienced outfitters who know what they are doing."

So I agreed to shut up, and that was probably where I made the mistake that created a real and genuine river-running adventure—as far as I was concerned.

It was mid-April, and our starting day dawned wet, cold and miserable at Lees Ferry, Arizona, which is the traditional shove-off point for river trips through the Grand Canyon. Our destination was Diamond Creek, a mere 225 miles down the big, brown, sullen-looking river. Several of the large, safe-looking pontoon rafts with outboard motors were tied up at the landing, and I began to feel better in spite of the wet snowflakes quietly melting down the back of my neck. Sunny Arizona?

We busily were packing and pushing our gear into small, waterproof packs when I looked up and saw through the snow a flotilla of small rafts come rowing down the river. To me they looked like tiny tenders or dinghies for servicing the regular rafts tied up in front of us, but these were our rafts. They were a short 17-feet long and designed to carry an oarsman amidship and four frightened passengers.

STOP THE RIVER, I WANT TO GET OFF

Have you ever seen a bug come sailing out of a water spout? Well, that's how I felt, and I'll never forget those 12 adventurous days of banging and bobbing about in the rough and roaring water with 45-degree rides up on curling waves that seemed higher than our raft was long.

Ye gods—how did I ever get in here? Frankly, I was wet, cold and scared for 12 days, but Ruby and Sue loved it. Halfway down the river I happened to recall that my old friend Joe Foss had only rolled his eyes a bit and smiled when I asked him about *his* canyon trip. I should have known that if you can bother General Joe . . . but it was too late now. And then there were long and welcome spells between rapids, spent at the oars or drifting silently as the river took us through the unbelievably beautiful canyon with only a narrow slit of blue sky seen through the towering walls above us. And so, as in all stories of the Colorado, we came to Lava Falls.

The rafts were all quietly huddled together on the beach above the thunder of the unseen Lava Falls rapids, a breathtaking inclined drop of 37 feet, roaring along for a quarter of a mile below us. The boatmen had gone down the river bank to look it over, and now they were coming back in solemn single file.

"How does it look, Steve?" I said.

"Big," he said without a smile.

This was their first attempt at Lava Falls with the smaller rafts, and they looked a little worried. If they are a little worried, I thought, how about us? I took another notch in my life preserver straps.

And big it was! We were the second boat down that 30-miles-per-hour roller coaster of raging white water with 15-foot waves towering over, around and on us. We made it. Two other boats didn't. They had flipped upside down, spilling their passengers into the rapids. Our boat was knee-deep in water as we sat there, half-stunned, at the foot of the rapids.

Then the boatman stood up and said "Bail! Damn it, bail! Get the water out of this boat. We've got people in the river!"

So bail we did. All you could see were rear ends and elbows. Fortunately, everyone got picked up, wet and a little shaken, but unharmed. I kissed my wife and daughter, and we all had a spot of strong liquid refreshment on the beach.

What a trip it was! Looking back now I owe the outfitter and all the friends we made a great debt of gratitude. So, wherever you all may be today—it's thanks again from the Mitchells and thanks, too, to the river and the canyon.   53

17 DO I REMEMBER SOUTH DAKOTA?

O I remember South Dakota in the good old days? Do I remember a limit of 17 ducks in the morning and 10 pheasants in the afternoon? I certainly do. So sit right down over there, here's a cup of coffee, and I'll tell you about it.

That's right—17 ducks and 10 pheasants. And the pheasant shooting hours didn't open until noon everyday. Geese? They are there now by the thousands, but they were mighty scarce in the late 30's—in Day County up in the northeastern corner of South Dakota. So scarce that it's no wonder I can still hear Sag Harris' old Model-T truck as it rattled to a halt after dark in front of the old clubhouse. He ran up the porch steps and called out to my Dad, "Clyde, there's geese in the country!"

That settled our hunting plans for the next day. Before dawn, we were traveling on prairie roads, heading for the field of wheat stubble or winter rye where a flock of Canada geese had been reported. Did we ever get any? Not many. In fact, I shot ducks and pheasants for 35 consecutive days one year and never got a shot at a goose. Thirty-five days? That's right, every single day from sunup till sundown. Got so accustomed to carrying my shotgun everywhere that after the season I couldn't get used to walking down the streets of my home town without it. Sort of like my wife and her everlasting purse.

Did I get to be a good shot? Well, my Dad won the World's Open Trapshooting Championship in 1931. He was a famous All-American pro, and it looks like I've spent my life proving that shooting ability isn't necessarily *hereditary*. But, I can tell you this about the last week of that long season after all that shooting, I didn't miss very much. The birds seemed to slow down, giving me plenty of time to shoot. You've heard about the great wing-shots of the past, and that's why they were great. There was a lot to shoot at.

Do I miss those days? Of course, but you finally realize that the size of the daily bag isn't what really counts. I've had just as good a day with one wise old cock pheasant as I might have had with 10 back then.

Where did all those South Dakota pheasants come from? The game management experts said it was due to the typical one-time population explosion of an exotic—or introduced—species coinciding with a phenomenal increase in suitable habitat. In other words, when there were lots of pheasant chicks hatched, there was lots of food for them to eat and lots of protective cover to hide in. It was during the Great Drought. The prairie potholes and sloughs were almost dry and had grown up in thick, high weeds for snug winter cover. The government had planted dwarf sunflowers to keep the land from blowing away, and this meant more food and cover. Many of the huge corn-fields we hunted had become overrun with seed-bearing weeds in the rows. "Dirty" cornfields we called them, and they were literally alive with feeding pheasants.

Seems hard to believe, but one year the local farmers petitioned the state to poison the pheasants. In the spring, the pheasants lined up behind the corn-planter and scratched up the kernels as fast as they were set in the ground. One day, I offered an old farmer, on whose land we had been hunting, a string of pheasants.

"Thanks, son", he said, "but I've been eating those dang things all year. My wife cans them." Times were tough.

Sure, the farmers hunted pheasants, sometimes right in the barnyard where the pheasants came to feed with their chickens. I've seen some great, unsung wing-shots in overalls. We always invited the farmers to hunt with us, and they often joined the party. The shells were on us, and spare guns, too.

The birds were never easy. These were wild, wiry, fast-running, fast-flying pheasants from the steppes of Mongolia. They flushed at our feet like a cock grouse or drove high over our heads with the prairie wind to put a ripple in their tail-feathers. They often sailed away unscathed.

Ducks? There wasn't much water left in the country that fall, so it concentrated the birds on small ponds scattered across the mud bottoms of what had once been an immense fresh-water lake. The migrating ducks piled into these ponds. Mostly gadwall, pintail, redhead, canvasback, bluebill and an occasional mallard. There was no cover around the puddles, so we pulled our skiff out over the mud and set up a portable blind and decoys. Hard going in waders, slogging and splashing through ankle-deep mud with a rope over our shoulders, dragging a skiff full of heavy wooden decoys, a roll-up blind, plenty of shells and our guns.

It was my Dad's idea one morning to get behind the skiff and push the stern with a paddle, while I bent almost double on a long pulling rope. All went well, until I stopped for breath and turned around to find my Dad, with a big grin, sitting comfortably in the skiff. I can still hear him laugh as I pulled off my cap and loudly protested his hitchhiking.

So many things I can still see and hear. There's something about a hunting trip that never really ends. All it takes is a question like yours about South Dakota to bring it all back. Here, let me freshen up your cup.

TURN
LEFT
AT THE
WATER TOWER
18

I

T was the early part of another duck season; we had just finished our first day of banging away at flocks of fast-flying bluebills on Pine Lake in northern Wisconsin. At the dock I asked Charlie Pierce who ran the camp: "Charlie, what happened to all the mudhens that were here last year?"

"Well, let's see now. They oughta be here about Friday," he answered.

"Friday!" I said. "They sent you a postcard?"

"No," he said calmly,"the coot will come in at night and be all over the lake by sunup." And, of course, that is exactly what happened . . . thousands of them.

I still wonder how those weak-flying, ungainly but good to eat "galloping ducks" we call a coot; those "water chicken" that can hardly get out of their own way, could fly miles in the dark just skimming the tops of the pines and splash down right on target to feed and rest when Charlie said they would. Talk about the swallows showing up at Capistrano on the same day year after year, it seemed to be happening at Pine Lake, too. But how *do* they do it?

There isn't a hunter among us who at sometime hasn't been confronted with the almost mind-boggling mysteries of bird migration. If you're a woodcock chaser like I am, you probably watch the fall calendar and the night sky for a full "Hunter's Moon" because we know full well that's just the ticket to bring in the flight birds from the North and fill the covers next morning with the whistles of flying woodcock and the collarbells of busy bird dogs. But now the scientific specialists in bird migration tell us that those Louisiana-bound timberdoodles fly just as well in the dark of the moon as they do when the yellow moon of the Hunter is in its fullest glory. How about that? And come to think of it, my Brittany and I have found flight birds in the alder thickets and marshy pockets on the morning after a moonless night.

The scientists also tell us that woodcock often repeat exactly the same migration route on their flight south, so if you think you've missed the same bird in the same spot two years in a row it's comforting to know that this is completely possible.

When I was young and bold and just out of school, I always quit whatever job I had in the fall and went hunting in South Dakota. This seemed, at the time, like a very sensible and reasonable thing to do and it wasn't until I got married that my views were abruptly changed. But my views of South Dakota have remained the same . . . the same special fondness for that great, wide-open land in which to roam about and hunt, and with days like that of "The Northern Flight" on the high prairies to remember. That was what both my Grandad and Dad called it, "The Northern Flight;" that massive migration of waterfowl moving south across the Dakotas.

And what a sight it was as my Dad and I crawled out of that battered old Oakland touring car on a deep-rutted black gumbo-mud road crossing the endless reaches of wheat stubble. We were coming back late from an afternoon of pheasant hunting when we saw that the "Northern Flight" was on. Dad reached in and turned off the clattering old engine, and it was suddenly very quiet as we stood there and looked. As far as you could see there were thousands of ducks in the air . . . moving south. All kinds of ducks—mallards, pintails, gadwall and tight little bunches of teal as far as you could see in every direction, and all this as the sun was going down in a quiet, golden prairie sky. Dad finally got back in the car and said, "I think we'll get an early start in the morning, son." And that's exactly what we did.

All of us know about homing pigeons and their remarkable ability to return like a feathered boomerang after they are carried miles away from their home coop. But did you hear about the experiment that proved once and for all that birds can be true navigators? In 1952, a single Manx shearwater, a long-winged seabird, was taken by a scientific group from its nesting burrow on the Skokholm Islands in Wales and sent "Air Ex-   59 press" to the Boston airport in Massachusetts where it was released. Without any direction from the Air Traffic Control Tower this shearwater took off immediately and 12½ days was back in its nesting burrow—grumbling, no doubt, about the interruption. The shortest possible Atlantic passage it could have flown was 3100 miles.

It is now believed—but, remember, not yet proven—that migrating birds have a built-in "time sense" which combined with their ability to use the sun by day and the stars and moon by night as guides somehow gets them there. It is also theorized that birds develop migrating techniques other than pure instinct and get to know their neighborhood from the air and if they lived long enough to make a trip or two along their flyways they recognize and respond to landmarks. So it's very possible that the big gander you saw leading a flock of Canada geese north this spring might have said to his troops, "O.K. gang. There's the water tower at Pottsville. Ready now—turn left" . . . and they were on their way to a few acres lost somewhere in the vast wildness of Canada, the nesting ground of their ancestors, or again they might have had only a short hop remaining to drop in on that pond at the edge of town where they nested last year. But big as a goose or little as that pair of barn swallows that insist on nesting again in your garage after a trip from their winter quarters in Argentina, they do come back . . . and it's spring again.

So when you add up all we know about migration and direction finding it's consoling to know that science and its everlasting, all-knowing computers hasn't yet been able to program precisely the subject "Migration, Birds" and give it a binary code number or its octal equivalent. It's good to know that a few profound mysteries still exist in this world . . . and as far as I'm concerned it still takes a big, full, yellow "Hunter's Moon" to produce a really good woodcock flight.

19 THE OLD MAN IN THE MARSH

I T wasn't turning into much of a duck day. The promising northwest wind that blew at sunup had soon died out to a few light puffs in the marsh, and the mid-afternoon sun felt warm and relaxing on Red Connel's back as he sat in his comfortable blind. Even Coot, the black Lab, was flat on his belly, enjoying the sun with only an occasional sharp-eared look around to check the horizon.

Red sighed deeply, pulled down his faded old khaki hunting cap over what had once been bright red hair, and settled down for a little nap. As he closed his eyes, he remembered how on a day like this he used to tell young Tommy (whom some people called "Little Red"), "Son, I need a little nap. You and Coot stand the watch. Call me if needed." And then Tommy would laugh and say, "Okay, Dad. We'll be watching."

As Red began to drift off, he suddenly heard the faint cry of Canada geese, and both he and Coot came awake to search the horizon. Coot saw them first and whined. A thin wavering line of geese, low out over the bay and heading for the marsh. He quickly switched from duck to goose loads and reached for his goose call. Then he waited. No need to call, for they were headed right at him. Coot was whining softly now as the geese came up over the far end of the marsh and began to climb. With an almost imperceptible tilt to their wings and talking all the while, they began a high and wide circle of the decoys. As they swung around behind him, he was startled by a loud, squealing and squawking noise that sounded like a barnyard goose caught in a fence. Then two shots were rapidly fired, and the geese flared off and were gone.

61

"What in the devil was that!" Red said aloud as both he and Coot stood up to look out over the back of the blind. Then he saw the source. No more than 75 yards behind him there was a bright green rowboat, half-pulled up in the cover, and a black-capped hunter with a double gun looking out over the bay at the fast disappearing geese.

Red overcame his sudden desire to shake his fist at his neighbor and then slumped back down in the blind muttering to himself about dumb hunters. First good Canadas he had seen. Really working, too. Of all the bum breaks. Looked like a kid, too. Shouldn't be allowed in the marsh.

Then Red heard the creak of oarlocks, and there was the young hunter. "Guess I shouldn't have shot at those geese," the teenage boy said wide-eyed, "But, they looked awful close."

"No you shouldn't have," Red growled. "They looked close because they're bigger than ducks. You're in my circle, too. And what in the world was all that racket you were making?"

"That's my new goose call," the boy said proudly and held it up for Red to see. "I've been practicing with my new record."

"Sounded to me like you need a new needle!" Red grunted. "Better get that god-awful green boat back in the cover and for the love-of-Mike take off that cap. You can see it a mile away."

"Yes sir," the boy said. "I only tried to make my boat grass color." After a few pulls on the oars, he pulled off his cap to reveal a flaming shock of bright red hair. He had gone only a few boat lengths when Red stood up and said, "On second thought, you'd better get in here with me. Then, I'll know where you are. Go hide that boat if you can, and I'll come pick you up."

After the brief visit of the geese, no more birds were moving, and the wind died down even more. The old man, the boy without his cap, and the dog sat silently looking out over the marsh. The nap, once postponed, began to seem attractive again to Red, and he finally said, "Keep your eyes open, young man. I'll take a little rest now. You and Coot are on watch."

Red was soon snoring softly in the warm sun, and fleeting pictures of another red-headed boy in the same blind drifted in and out of his dreams. Then he felt the boy nudging his arm as he whispered, "Sir, I've been counting the duck decoys, and we've got too many. The dog seems to think so, too." Red slowly opened his eyes, peered out from under the visor of his pulled down cap, and saw three black ducks sitting necks up on the edge of the decoys.

"Are you ready?" Red said. "On your side now. Let's go."
As they got to their feet, the pair sprang up on Red's side, and
the single went to the boy. Three shots and three fat black
ducks were down. A double for Red and a single for the boy.
"Holy cow, mister; I got one," the boy said excitedly. "And
you got 'em both. Wow! A double! You must be an expert."
"At times, boy. At times," Red said with a small smile.

Later on, back at the boat landing, Red waited for the boy to
come rowing in off the marsh, and with the setting sun behind
him his hair looked redder than ever. Red pulled the nose of the
boat up on the bank and threw in two of the ducks. "Enough
for a meal," he said. "Gee, thanks again, mister. My mother will
be mighty pleased. And I'll pick yours, too. My dad showed me
how a long time ago, but he's not home any more. I'll bring
them over tonight. I know where you live."

"You do?" Red asked.

"Yes sir, Mr. Connel. I saw Coot and your duck boat in the
backyard just after we moved here in August. My name is Steve
Benson."

"Okay, Steve. See you later."

That evening Red heard Coot bark and looked out on the
lighted back porch to see him greet Steve and nose the package
he was carrying. Steve said, "Hello," and handed Red two
neatly picked ducks.

"Why two?" Red asked.

"Well, sir, I got to thinking about that double, and they sort
of really belong to you."

"Now, Steve," Red said firmly. "Take 'em both. No more
discussion. You hear me!"

"Yes sir. Thanks very much," Steve said, and as he went to
leave, Red stopped him with, "Weather report says strong
northwest wind tomorrow. If you can be on time, I might see
you at the landing before daybreak.

"Yes sir, I'll be on time. I found my dad's old hunting cap, too.
Maybe I should go down and sleep in the boat."

"That won't be necessary," Red laughed. "Good night, boy."

"Who was that?" his wife Martha said as he went back into
the kitchen.

"Steve Benson. A kid I met in the marsh today."

"For a minute he sounded like Tommy," Martha said. After
a long pause she added, "I worry about your hunting alone
every day. Couldn't you find a hunting partner?"

"Maybe I have, Martha. Maybe I have."

63

20 BEN GOES HOME

EVERYBODY in our town wondered how John Gardner was going to convince his new bride, Mary, that the proper place for a good bird dog was in the house. Mary was a "house-proud" Jensen, and her dad used to complain that if he didn't shut the front gate, Mary and her mother would sweep at least a half-mile of the road on both sides of the house.

So when John brought home the new English setter pup, Ben, as a surprise birthday present for Mary, we heard that things didn't quite work out as John had planned. After the first long night of the pup's loud and lonely yelps, including his several mistakes on Mary's gleaming and antiseptic kitchen floor, Ben ended up in the woodshed.

Like his father before him, John and I have always opened the grouse season together. It was a good day, and the young and eager Ben showed all the signs of becoming another fine Gardner grouse dog. Somehow, he seemed to know what we were trying to do. His beautiful, high-tailed, high-headed gait made John grin with pride.

My old Rex dog made the first point, but when Ben beat him to the retrieve, I thought Rex was going to tackle him. Instead, Rex just looked back at me, and if dogs can shrug their shoulders, that's what he did. Much as if to say, "What the hell. Youth will be served."

When we got back to John's house just before sundown, Mary was standing on the back porch waving "hello." When I opened the back of the stationwagon, Ben jumped out with a grouse in his mouth. He trotted across the yard, up the porch steps and laid the bird at Mary's feet. She leaned over as though to pat him, then seemed to change her mind and disappeared into the house. John stared at the closed door.

"She almost petted him that time, didn't she?" he said softly. He asked me in for a drink, but it was getting dark.

"Thanks, John, another time," I said.

It doesn't seem possible that a disagreement over whether a dog should sleep in the kitchen or the woodshed could lead to a serious domestic rift. John didn't talk much about it on our Saturday hunts, but I had a hunch something was wrong.

As luck would have it, business took me out of town for two weeks right smack in the middle of hunting season. When I got home on Friday night, my wife told me, with tears in her eyes, that John and Mary had split up. Trial separation, or something like that. John and Ben had moved into the old Martin place; Mary was all alone in her clean and spotless house.

When I called John about our Saturday hunt, he said, "Sure, let's go. Usual time okay?"

"I'll see you then," I said and hung up.

It was late in the season and plenty cold. With not much cover left, it turned into a long hunt for the two birds we took. The sun was setting when we turned in at the Martin place. John let Ben out of the car and asked me in for a drink. I wanted to get home and into a hot bath, but knowing how he must feel about that dark and silent house, I just couldn't turn him down. It was cold in the bare kitchen. He switched on the light and swung open the refrigerator door.

"Here's a bachelor's ice-box for you," he said. "A six-pack of beer and a bottle of ketchup."

John took a few sips of his beer. Then he went to the door and whistled for Ben, but Ben must have had other things on his mind. We sat there, quietly drinking our beer in that cold kitchen, when the phone rang. John leaned over the table and picked it up. As he listened, his face fell.

Then, "No, of course I didn't send him over there. I've just been whistling for him. Yes, I know he had to cross the turnpike. I'm sorry about your floor. Put the bird and the dog on the porch. Okay. I'll come and get him."

He hung up, looked at me for a moment, and then shook his head. "Would you believe it? That crazy pup took one of those grouse back to Mary. Tracked up her clean floor. She's really mad—and half crying." He rose from the table. "There's more beer, so don't go. I'll be right back."

66   But, of course, he wasn't right back. When I drove by Mary's

house on the way home, John's car was in the driveway. Ben wasn't sitting on the porch, so he must have been inside too.

Now, it seems pretty far-fetched to credit Ben with planning the Gardner reconciliation—that's going too far. But when my wife and I visited John and Mary last week, the first thing Mary did was take us all out to the kitchen. There was Ben, right next to the stove in his shiny new dog box with an honest-to-goodness mail order dog mattress.

"Things have certainly changed," I said. Mary smiled, "As an old hunter, you should know *never* to underestimate the power of a good bird dog."

Ben came out to greet us, and after a few pats, including one from Mary, walked back to his box, flopped down and looked around at all of us in that warm, bright kitchen. He stretched slowly and with one big sigh of contentment, curled up and went to sleep.

WILL SKEET SHOOTING SPOIL A GOOD HUNTER? 21

I T was a hot, cloudless July day in the midst of the "World's Skeet Championship," in Rochester, N.Y., more than a few years ago—about 1966. Jimmy Robinson, famous and inimitable scribe of clay target sports, was napping in his chair on the clubhouse porch. I walked by and gently nudged his outstretched legs. Jimmy slowly tilted back his hat.

"What's up, Jack?"

"Got a story for you. Just walked past field 12 and saw a shooter miss one."

"Well, that's something," Jimmy replied with a straight face. "Did you get his name?"

"No, but they stopped the squad while the officials talked to him. He promised not to do it again, and they let him continue."

Jimmy chuckled, lowered his hat brim and resumed his nap. Of course, Jimmy Robinson would be the first to deny that skeet is an easy game, because it's *not*. What we were both kidding about were the incredible scores the shooters were posting in 1966. And now, in 1978, just in case you haven't heard about it, Walt Badorek from Klamath Falls, Ore., won the World's All-Around Title at San Antonio with 550 × 550. A perfect score. In other words, he never missed a single official target all week, including 100 straight with the 410, 28 and 20-gauge, and 250 straight with the 12-gauge.

Unless you shotgun hunters have actually tried a round or two of *regulation* skeet—not just hand-trap practice—it's easy to

68

ask "Yeah, but how do these mechanical hotshots do in the field?" The other man's game often appears easy. But there is a definite relationship between gun handling, pointing and swinging at a flying clay target and doing the same on a feathered target. The principles are the same. If you can hit a respectable number of orthodox skeet targets, chances are that you can do pretty well in the field.

But that's not always the story. "Rock" Rohlfing of the National Shooting Sports Foundation once told me about a well-known skeet expert who could break a hundred straight without half trying, but never could put it together in the hunting field. The reason? Believe it or not, he never knew *when* to shoot. The first time they hunted together a grouse busted out in front of Rock and flew to the skeet champ's side. It was his bird, but he didn't shoot. Instead he turned to Rock and complained, "But you didn't say 'Mark'!"

Another venerable hunter and skeet champion, 76-year-old Henry Alcus, who shoots with my hunting partner, Alex Stott, every year at the Great Eastern Skeet Championships, broke 100 straight on two consecutive days at this shoot last June. That's 200 straight. When his teammate, Dave Crosby, asked how he did it, Henry said "Just plain luck. I don't seem to have the same reactions I had when I was 75."

I once found myself with a distinguished pair of shotgun champions on a Wisconsin ruffed grouse hunt, Vic Reinders and Ed Scherer. Vic had just won the North American Clay Target Championship in trapshooting and Ed was the World's 20-Gauge Skeet Champion. If they had worn all their medals and brassards, they wouldn't have been able to get out of my Dad's car up there on the La Crosse River.

The plan was to hunt along the river for a while, then head west eight or ten miles to another road where Dad would pick us up. Away we went behind Ed's fine pointer Dollar, a wide-ranging, Texas-bred, bird-finder. The pace soon turned into what seemed to me a full gallop. The cry was "Point!" Bam. One bird—one bam. "Point!" Two birds—two bams. Didn't these guys ever miss? Then we waded the river like Robert's Rangers, crossing and recrossing the La Crosse.

After we'd gone what seemed 20 or 30 miles, most of it in the river, and I'd fired one parting shot at a tree-top high grouse, I managed to catch up with the main body of the hunt.

"Fellows," I panted, "no complaints, but I don't seem to be getting very much shooting."

"That," Vic said, "is because you don't shoot very much. You've got to stay up with the dog."

And that's what I tried to do—almost at a dead run. Finally I was there when "Dollar" locked up on a big cock grouse. He came out on my side, and somehow I downed him. Then both of these world champions looked down from their Olympian heights, smiled and said, almost in unison, "Good shot, Jack." The trip was made.

When we got out to the far road, Dad was there waiting for us. "How'd you shoot?" he asked.

"Averaged about two shots to a bird," I replied.

It was a good average, and after all, he didn't ask me how many birds. But, somehow, I think he knew.

Looking back now on that hunt with the champs, it was a pleasure to see that Ed Scherer's son, John, now in the U. S. Air Force, broke 100 × 100 in both the 410 and 28-gauge at this year's World's Skeet Championships. I'm not really surprised. I remember Ed's story of how John, when he was just a little guy, "practiced skeet" regularly with his pop-gun, calling out "Pull" and "Bang" and swinging away in the kitchen. One day he stopped, put his gun down and said, "I missed one."

"Why?" his Dad asked.

"Raised my head," John said.

So before you dismiss skeet-shooting as a purely mechanical exercise with little relation to flying birds, you'd better try it. And, above all, don't bet that a good skeet shot can't hit game. If you do, you may go home with your pockets emptied.

FUNDAMENTALLY, I'M A GOOD SHOT

22

DID you ever meet a hunter who admits he's a bum shot? I've met plenty of golfers, for example, who readily admit to being just a hacker. "But I like the exercise," they say. But no hunter admits he's a hacker. We're all *fundamentally good shots,* but lots of things come up. Bad gun fit is the worst. Tight jackets, too. "Did you see that? The son-of-a-gun flew right into the sun!" And another one, "I was waiting for you to shoot, so I just threw in a snap shot."

And when it comes to riflemen, did you ever notice how many of them, after a mysterious miss, are the innocent victims of "someone's been monkeying with this scope adjustment" or "that bump in the gun rack must have knocked my sights cockeyed." Your comment, "I think you closed both eyes" is better left unsaid.

Trap and skeet shooters aren't much better, either. I thought I had heard every alibi in the book but I just ran into a new one. This trap shooting friend of mine made the mistake of trying out his new shooting glasses in competition and shot miserably. When I tried to console him he said "It's these damn glasses! I was shooting at a speck on the right lens and everything looked like a straightaway." That could happen. Strange things make a difference. One of my worst shooting days—and I've had some bad ones—was entirely due to forgetting to wear my lucky shoelaces.

On the other hand, when you do have a good day in the hunting field with no need for a single alibi, what proof do you have of your performance? If you're shooting targets, you have the score or perhaps even a trophy, but no one seems to remember that long, clean rifle shot you made, or that shotgun double or just a string of good singles. Of course, you always have your hunting companions to rely on, but somehow they don't seem to have the same zest or ring of truth that you have in recounting your personal prowess.

Now, I have a unique solution for handling those rare days of excellence to be sure they are indelibly recorded. Here is how I happened to develop this new method of documenting unusual performance in the field.

It was December, 1973, at the Remington Arms Annual Gun-Writer's Seminar. I was lucky enough to be mule-deer hunting with the Mescalero Apache Indians on their big reservation near Ruidoso, New Mexico. For some reason or other, I remembered that Geronimo's name means "One Who Yawns" when I met my Apache guide, Leon Botella, the next morning and began to talk Wisconsin deer hunting to this quiet, professional hunter. Always polite, but somehow amused and a little bored with all of our mighty paleface preparations for the hunt, he seemed particularly amused when I tried a few sighting-in-shots with my Remington 7mm mag.

You see I really do have this arthritis in my neck, I could show you the X rays, (as well as a very tight jacket) and even with a rest and sling across the hood of his pickup truck, my attempts to hit a large white rock up on the mountain were not very impressive.

"You flinch a little bit," he said.

"No," I answered, "I merely over-anticipate recoil."

The guide looked at me and said quietly, "Can you walk OK?"

Can I walk OK! How about that? Sure I can walk OK, and I figured that I would show him how to walk OK. What a mistake. Leon bounced ahead of me like a rubber ball up and down the ridges. At about 7000 feet, I was soon acting like a punctured beach raft—hissing loudly and about to fold up in a mass of wrinkles.

Then Leon suddenly stopped, pointed up the steep side of the sloping ridge and said, "There he is . . . lying down. See him, under the tree?"

Under what tree? I tried them all and finally saw only the flick of a mule-deer's ear and the point of a horn. Well over 250 yards, at least, I thought. So I collapsed into my sling and the proper prone position and saw nothing but brush. I tried sitting, then kneeling and still nothing.

So I finally rose unsteadily to my feet and wobbled about while Leon kept saying, "You better shoot. You better shoot. He sees us."

The scope and my breathing began to settle down, and I finally saw the deer. I thought the next time the ears and horn float by in the scope I'll try it—and I did.

"You got him," Leon shouted. "Good shot!"

It *was* about 250 yards, paced off, but strangely enough no one seemed to believe me when I returned in quiet triumph to the cocktail party in Ruidoso where all the gun writers attending the seminar assembled. It had been a big day, with lots of deer taken, and I had a hard time waiting for the opportune time to casually mention my off-hand, seeing the ears and one horn only, uphill, spectacular, 250-yard, one-shot kill. And when I finally told my story I was greeted with only an "Is that so?" nod from such famous riflemen and gun-writers as Jim Carmichel, Charlie Askins, Elmer Keith and the like. They just looked at me and rattled the ice in their glasses.

So, the next day, I cornered Leon at the Mescalero headquarters and he signed, with a big smile, the following statement:

To Whom it May Concern:
250 yards. Uphill. Buck lying down.
One shot—off hand by Jack Mitchell.
Witness: Leon H. Bottela, Guide,
December 13, 1973

Richard A. Wardlaw, a government official at the reservation, formally notarized the sworn statement and affixed his official seal with an even bigger smile than Leon's. Somehow, no one seemed to take the whole matter too seriously. Nor did the gun writers accord the notarized statement exactly the proper respect I had hoped for when I confronted them with it that evening. But one of the old-timers, after a laugh and a shake of the head, called everyone to attention and said, "OK guys. You've got to listen to Jack's story now. It's been *notarized!"*

23 HOW TO COOK, CHEW & SWALLOW WILD GAME

SOME wag once said, "Nostalgia certainly isn't what it used to be."

Fortunately, there is one thing that certainly isn't what it used to be, that is the state of the art of cooking wild game. I say "fortunately" because, in my opinion, the modern concepts and methods of game cookery are far ahead of even the most traditional dishes of the past. So before some of you old-timers start shaking your fists at me, let me explain.

As the popularity of cookbooks on every conceivable subject from truffle-stuffing to lettuce soup grew over the years, there were bound to be books and articles on how to cook wild game better. And now we have them. One explains how to marinate a woodchuck, and another in the Remington cookbook gives a recipe for moose stroganoff. When I first read that recipe, I thought they were talking about a linebacker for the Green Bay Packers, but it's a very special way to cook moose. I tried it and it's delicious.

Memories and stories about cooking game and campfire recipes come back to me easily whenever I give them a chance. Take, for instance, the relatively simple chore of making coffee outdoors. A cowpuncher friend of mine has claimed for years that a pot of special campfire coffee I brewed absolutely ruined a new pair of hair chaps he was wearing. He claims he spilled

75

only a few drops of my coffee on one leg, and the next day all the hair fell out—on both legs.

I was never what you might call a good camp cook. (When I read this to my wife, she corrected me by saying, "You were never what you might call a *cook!*"). But I did turn out some pretty unusual products in my time. Products that, had I persevered in their development, might have made history.

Take, for example, a batch of venison jerky I once made. To my amazement, the more I chewed this jerky the *bigger* it got. What's more, it was delicious. Think what this multiplying meat might have meant to the protein-starved world. I tried to duplicate it several times but failed, and my friends and their jaws got tired of the experiments. My four-way stretch pancakes had great promise as well, but that's another story.

Living off the land and by the gun is a fond dream of many of us. Years ago, both my grandfather and father had the chance to try it. Storm-bound and marooned for three days on an island in Johnson's Lake up in Canada, they had nothing to eat but the ducks they had shot. No bacon, no bread and no coffee. Just lake water and campfire-roasted duck—without salt. On the third day, in order to relieve the monotony of their diet, they had teal for breakfast, mallard for lunch and canvasback for dinner. I can remember my dad saying that for a long time after their rescue just the sound of a duck-call gave him heartburn.

Moving to Connecticut from the Midwest with memories of corn-fed mallards and canvasbacks in wild celery, I found it hard to get used to eating saltwater ducks. I am not about to repeat that old saw about "throwing out the coot and eating the brick" but there were lots of recipes for coot.

To freshwater waterfowl hunters, a coot is a mudhen. But to a New Englander, it's the scoter—a big hard-flying, hard-to-stop sea duck that lives on clams and fish. I once asked one of these scoter hunters how you prepared them for the table.

"Fix 'em with dandelion wine," he said.

"You mean you marinate them in the wine?" I asked.

"Nope. You drink the wine. About four big water glasses full will do it. Then you sit right down and eat the coot. Mighty good, too!"

If you're collecting unusual recipes for shotgun game, I could refer you to my young hunting friend, Miley Bull. The dish is Borneo fruit bat. First, you must spend, as Miley did, six months in the jungles of Borneo on a scientific expedition, live mostly on rice and become very interested in a change of menu. Miley's companions were the native Muruts, and they consider this flying mammal, with its 18-inch wing span and fruit diet, to be a rare delicacy. Specially prepared in a Chinese wok with some wild jungle vegetables, Miley managed to eat one whole bat.

When asked how it was, Miley said, "Absolutely awful!" Evidently, you must acquire a taste for Borneo fruit bat.

As kids, we always looked forward to my grandfather's tales of waterfowl hunting in Canada. One of his often-told stories involved a big old whistling swan which was legal game in those days.

"Took a day to pick it and two days to cook it," he said.

"Was it tough, Grandad?" we always asked.

"Was it *tough?*" he answered. "Even the gravy was tough!" Then how we all laughed.

It looks as though most of these stories are concerned with culinary disasters, but there is a good reason for it. I'm on a diet. If I start to recall the smell of venison chops and deer liver coming from the cook shanty of some almost-forgotten deer camp or remember the fragrance of sharp-tailed grouse bubbling away in a dutch oven nestled in the hot ashes of a campfire, I'm lost. A head-long charge to the refrigerator will be inevitable. I know where my wife hid some cold smoked pheasant.

MY WAR WITH THE 24 INSECT WORLD

AS a very young man, I stood quietly on a high granite ledge looking out on the head of magnificent Knife Lake in the Quetico-Superior canoe wilderness. A lone woodsman, I was wearing a big head-net draped from a broad-brimmed straw hat and puffing furiously, with some intermittent gulping, on a borrowed, ancient and encrusted black-briar pipe stuck through a hole in the net. The clouds of acrid pipe smoke and sparks that I was over-producing were supposed to fight off the swarms of god-awful black flies that hung silently in the air about me.

I stood there and in my youthful imagination saw the ghosts of the old French voyageurs. Their big freight canoes were laden down with beaver pelts as they passed by with flashing blades on the long paddle and portage down from Hudson's Bay. I was really playing a part and saw myself as a figure on the cover of an outdoor magazine. That was until I suddenly got sick from the pipe and my hat caught on fire.

Seems like I've spent a lot of time in the out-of-doors trying to stop some insect from drilling me for blood, jabbing me with its stinger or laying its eggs under my hide. I remember most of them, but like the black flies of the Quetico, there have been some insects that are as fresh in my memory as a 10-point buck or a six-pound brook trout would be.

There was that swarm of deer flies in Wyoming that started it all—or maybe they were moose flies. The moose fly, my father once claimed, was the fly that "bites a chunk out of your neck and then lights up on your ear to eat it." Like a hawk with a dead pigeon.

The place was Slough Creek, and I was intently watching my brother Bob's dry fly floating back to me as I cautiously waded around a bend in the creek. And there he was! Lying belly down in the cool water to escape the biting flies was the largest bull moose in the world, bar none. He slowly raised his gigantic head and 14-foot antlers to look at me. Then he began to get up—and up—to his feet. With the water cascading off his massive shoulders, the moose looked at least 40 to 50 feet tall. So tall that I had to tilt back my shaking head to look up at him. His red eyes, the size of basketballs, were glowing down at me with a horrible hatred of all mankind, especially dumb trout fishermen who disturb his naps in the creek.

Armed only with a four-ounce fly rod, I decided against a direct frontal attack and chose to retreat, as casually as possible. I slowly reeled in my line, cringing at the loud click of the reel, sat the fly carefully in the cork of the handle and began my retreat. Did you ever try to stroll *backwards* in a creek? Finally I turned around and attempted again to saunter slowly back down the creek. Was he following me? I couldn't look. Then I heard splashing. That was too much. Throwing my rod up on the bank and scrambling after it, I headed for a clump of willows on the edge of the meadow. Heavy boot-foot waders are made for wading, not for running in tall grass. Ignoring this fact and hearing the snorts of the moose right behind me, I touched ground only once or twice in my 100-yard dash to the willows. Once there I whirled around, wide-eyed, for a final showdown and saw the moose, somehow much smaller in size, still standing in the creek, looking curiously in my direction. As I watched, still breathing hard, he wandered away up the meadows. After some search, I found my fly rod and went home.

That whole embarassing incident would never have happened, except for those damned deer flies—or maybe they were moose flies.

My real insect enemy, however, is the miserable mosquito. Mosquitoes wait for me to arrive and then they send up a signal flare. "He's here!" they say.

In spite of the best repellents, I've been chewed on in the Arctic summertime, bitten fiercely in East Africa and India, gnawed without mercy in the jungles of the Amazon and stung sharply and incessantly on the marshy flats of New Jersey. As many of you well know, the famous mosquitoes of New Jersey *are* bigger. A camper friend of mine swears that he woke up in his tent one night and there were two Jersey mosquitoes standing at the foot of his cot. One mosquito said to the other, "Shall we carry him away, or shall we eat him here?"

But the mosquitoes I will never forget—or forgive—are the giant sabertoothed, bloodthirsty female mosquitoes (it's only the female that bites) that live at the mouth of Mosquito Creek (where else?) on the Bogachiel River in the rain forests of Washington's Olympic Peninsula. Humming clouds of these predators wait for you there in the hanging moss.

My wife and I were backpacking up the Bogachiel, and Mosquito Creek was our first night out. In the interest of lighter packs, we had decided that one sleeping bag was really big enough for two. It was—almost. The "almost" was my ample posterior around which the zipper of the bag absolutely refused to go. I became a living target for those dive-bombing devils. On top of the mosquitoes, we had evidently made camp smack in the middle of an elk trail. All night long those Olympic elk would approach us, snort and break off into the bush.

It was a very long night punctuated with frightened elk, soft curses and back-side slapping. My wife slept well.

After all this I'm beginning to itch a little, so I will now stand up at my typewriter. I might even scratch a bit, politely, of course. Like all these old memories, those bites seem to last a long time.

25 YOU MISSED ALL THE EXCITEMENT

EVERYONE in our town knew and respected Miss Myra Whittaker. Many of us well remembered what a stern and unrelenting taskmaster she had been when we first confronted the mind-numbing mysteries of high school algebra. It was quite a while ago, but to this day I've never been quite sure what "x" is equal to or why anyone should really want to know. "Mental discipline," Miss Whittaker said.

She had a great regard for discipline and order. Her famous flower and vegetable garden at the house where she lived alone was an example. A wandering, carefree weed or a carrot with bad posture that showed up in her rigid rows never had a chance. And woe betide the dog, out for a stroll, that dared to set a friendly foot in Miss Whittaker's garden. Met with feminine shrieks and the wallops of a broom, the bewildered visitor ran at least an extra 100 yards in retreat before he sat down, looked back in amazement and wondered what in the world he had done.

When Miss Whittaker retired from teaching, she was given a fine party, including all kinds of speeches and a framed plaque and testimonials to what she had meant to the town and her students. After it was over though, she sort of dropped out of things. We saw her working in her garden and walking alone to church, but that was about all.

No one quite knew why the pretty Myra Whittaker had never married, but my wife who had lived next door to the Whittaker house when she was growing up remembered that

81

Myra had once had a steady beau named Ben Faber. This suitor, according to my wife, was a big, angular, smiling young man who always had a hunting dog of some kind at his heel. Ben loved to hunt and fish. And with the very proper, hard-working Whittaker family, this was where the trouble all started. You know it wasn't so long ago that anyone who spent too much time with a gun or a fishing rod in his hand was sort of suspect. It was obviously a carry-over from our Puritan ancestors who devoutly believed that only work was Godly and that the devil himself ran with the hounds. Did you ever notice that in the old pictures of the "First Thanksgiving Feast" only the Indians bringing in the game seem to be happy. The Puritans all look like they are itching to get back to the fields and pick some more pumpkins.

So Ben Faber and his dog were no longer seen at the Whittaker house. No one seems to remember how young Myra felt about all this. My wife, who often takes the unusual view, said she thinks that Myra's reaction to a dog in her garden is a reaction to her past.

"Chasing away a memory," my wife says sadly.

With all this as a background, you can imagine the astonishment of the neighbors when one bright September morning Miss Whittaker, in her proper hat and white gloves, came out through the front gate with a frisky, long-legged English setter bouncing about on the end of a new leash. Seems that the pup, Sarah, had belonged to her favorite niece who had spent the summer out at the Whittaker cottage on the lake and now was away at school with no place to keep a dog. Somehow she had convinced her Aunt Myra to take the dog. Everyone was amazed.

I was doing some travelling for my company in those days, and at the end of a two-week trip I returned home to find my wife bursting with the news.

"Ben Faber is back in town," she said.

"Ben who?" I asked.

"Ben Faber, Miss Whittaker's old beau! It's just like the movies," she said smiling.

"Where has he been?" I asked.

"Alaska. He's a civil engineer or something, and now he has come back here to retire. He's single and the first thing he did was call on Myra."

"That should satisfy you," I said. "And now they can all live happily ever after."

"Well, not exactly," my wife said seriously. "Ben borrowed Myra's dog to go hunting, and she got into a skunk plus a lot of cockle-burrs and mud."

"And Myra chased both of them out of the garden with a broom," I said laughing.

"No, and it isn't funny either," my wife objected. "But whatever happened, Ben hasn't been back to the house since."

On my return from the next trip my wife met me at the door with a wide smile.

"We are invited to the wedding," she said happily. "And you missed all the excitement."

"What happened?" I asked.

"Myra's dog ran away. She just disappeared one night. Myra was beside herself and called Ben, and he hunted for her all night, and it was a bitter cold one. For three days and nights that crazy Ben hunted for Sarah.

"Well, what happened?" I said anxiously.

"He found her. Way up north. She'd cut her leg, but she was all right. I was there at Myra's when he came up on the back porch with Sarah in his arms. They were both all wet and muddy—and bloody from the cut."

"Then what?" I said.

"I'm not quite sure but Myra suddenly broke down when she saw them. She cried and hugged and kissed Ben. There wasn't much I could do so I just came home. I really don't think they even heard me say 'good-bye'."

As a final note I'd like to report that Ben and I got to be hunting partners and that Sarah turned out to be one of the finest bird dogs I've ever shot over. And the last time I went by their house, Sarah was sound asleep in a bed of Myra's prize petunias.

26 BACK TO WHERE THE HEATHER GROWS

ARK TWAIN once said that it isn't what people know that causes trouble, it's what they know that isn't so that really makes for problems. Unfortunately, so many of us here in this country have some strange preconceived notions about other countries and other people.

In spite of the fact that both my great grandparents came from Scotland, I had only my boyhood memories of the scratchy old phonograph records that brought Sir Harry Lauder and his broad Scottish burr into my grandparent's parlor singing "Back, Back To Where The Heather Grows." He was the stereotyped Scot with tam o'shanter, kilts, a crooked walking stick, bagpipes and a wee dram of whisky. But most of the Scots we knew about, or thought we knew about, were dour, silent people living in a cold and rainy country and tight-fisted enough to make Jack Benny seem like a spendthrift.

My wife and I, thanks to a group of my friends, have just returned from "where the heather grows." Many of the things I thought I knew about Scots and Scotland are just not so.

First, the *Scots* (not the Scotch—the only time you use that word is for "Scotch" whisky or "Scotch" broth) are some of the most friendly, generous, cordial and kind people I've ever met. What's more, they seem to especially like Americans. The country is big, clean, beautiful and rugged with people to match.

Another word like "Scotch" that you must use with discretion in Great Britain is "hunting." An old friend, Jim Dee, on

85

his first trip over there, casually mentioned to his host that he might like to do some hunting, thinking, of course, of guns and game. The next morning Jim was awakened by the clatter of horses' hooves on the cobblestones below his bedroom window. There, to his astonishment, was the entire local "hunt" with fox hounds, horns, horses and pink-coated riders waiting to welcome him. How Jim explained his mistake in not using the term "shooting" for what we Americans call "hunting" is not quite clear, but he thanked them very kindly and did not join the hunt.

"Tell me, Mr. MacGregor," I said. "How is the deer hunting here in the Highlands?"

"The *what*, sir?" he said. "Oh, you mean the deer*stalking*. Quite good. If you are in shape for it."

Mr. MacGregor said that with a quick but obvious glance at my waist-line. Pulling in my stomach as far as possible, I was about to tell him of the long, cold hours I had strenuously spent sitting on deer stands in Wisconsin when I remembered what Dr. Frank Serena, experienced American big game hunter, had told me about stalking the red deer stag in Scotland.

"If you think," Doc said, "that you just stroll around in the heather-covered hills dressed in knickers and a two-way hat with a canny old Scot that leads you directly to a pre-selected stag, you are wrong."

"I always thought somehow that it was a highly accepted but exclusive ritual designed for Belgian counts and the English nobility," I said, "the real sport of kings, but comfortable."

"Wrong again. Toughest hunt I ever made. No tree cover on those bare Highland hills. You try to get above the stag. Spooky as an elk. Low profile and no skylining. So you and your gillie spend hours crawling on your hands and knees and often on your belly in the mud and the heather. Low profile—like a snake."

The other traditional shooting that always intrigued me was the famous red grouse of Scotland. Again, I had my preconceived notions about big kills of driven birds with beaters, loaders, shooting butts, matched pairs of fancy double guns and all the traditional trappings enjoyed by the guests on Lord Sidebottom's moor. It looked as though the grouse didn't have much of a chance. And that's what I thought until Ian Mac Quarrie and I were walking up over the hill in a cold, gray drizzle on our way to try the trout at Fishnish Lochs.

Suddenly I was startled by a winged something that whistled

over our heads like a feathered bullet and disappeared in the fog.

"What in the world was that?" I asked.

"That, my friend," he laughed, "was a grouse."

No wonder Dave Crosby says, "They're the toughest game bird I ever shot at. They can change speed and direction without missing a wing beat. The real trick when the driven birds come flying at you is to take the first bird far enough out in front in order to get off another shot before they are over your head and away. Then the loader slaps another double gun into your hands for the going-away shots."

Dave, in my opinion, is one of the best all-around shotgun pointers in the business. So when he says "toughest game bird I ever shot at" you'd better listen.

If it were at all possible to mention fishing in this magazine, I might be tempted to tell you about the gigantic Scottish salmon I hooked by mistake on my two-ounce trout rod.

"No salmon will take in that area," they said.

They were wrong. As far as I know that big salmon is still going back to the sea—all the way down the big, brown, rolling, rainy River Tay. I never even stopped him. But this is a hunting magazine, and I refuse to tell you about it. Not a single word.

OLD DOGS 27

I can well remember when Old Man Wilson was Mr. Jim Wilson, one of the best wing shots and bird dog handlers in these parts. Several of us kids in town used to ride our bikes out to see him when he was working around his place. His wife, Martha, would always welcome us with a plate of home-made cookies. If Mr. Wilson wasn't too busy, he'd take us into his den to see the guns and the pictures of famous bird dogs that he had shot over and in some cases actually handled on the field trial circuit. Grouse dogs were his specialty, and he always had at least four or five pointers and setters in his kennels to show us. There was also a noisy little cocker spaniel, named Jiggs, that greeted us at the house.

The Wilsons had two daughters who had gone east to school. Both had married well and were living somewhere near New York City. They didn't get back home very often, but Mr. and Mrs. Wilson always made a point of showing us their pictures.

All my boyhood memories of the Wilsons were happy ones. Years later when I moved back to my home town, I was sorry to hear that Martha had died and that Jim was living alone in that big house. He was known as Old Man Wilson now, but not to his face. I heard that he had never quite recovered from the loss of his wife and had become more silent and withdrawn from the world with each passing year of loneliness. He no longer hunted, and the kennel was empty. All those great dogs were gone.

Bill Devers, my boyhood friend was one of the few people that Jim would still see. Most callers never found him at home. The sound of the big brass knocker echoed through the lonely house. No dog barked a welcome and no one came to the door. Evidently Jim Wilson just wanted to stay in his house and be left alone.

That winter, Jim had the flu, and his daughters and their husbands came to see him. We heard from Doc Thompson that, after he was getting better, the daughters wanted Jim to sell the house and move to an Arizona retirement community near where one of the daughters had a winter home. This plan, according to Doc, got a real rise out of Jim, and he said he wasn't about to spend his last days "in a corduroy leisure suit playing shuffleboard."

One of the sons-in-law suggested that Jim get a dog for companionship and Jim stopped that one too. He said "The only dog I'd want would be a bird dog, and I'm too old to start a new one."

Jim recovered from the flu but not from his despondency. Early that fall Bill Devers asked me to come along on one of his visits. When we drove up, Bill was surprised to see Jim out of the house, sitting on the front porch. Before Bill could tell Jim who I was he said, "Sorry we're all out of cookies."

We shook hands, and although I couldn't help notice how old and bent he looked, I was glad to feel his firm grip and see the sparkle in his eye. He certainly didn't look like a downcast old duffer that morning. Bill must have noticed it too, because he said, "Jim, what have you been doing to yourself? You look great."

Jim grinned and said "I've got a new bird dog!"

"Is it a pup?" I asked.

Jim laughed and said "Not exactly. Come on out to the kennels, and I'll show her to you."

As we started down the steps, Bill picked up Jim's cane that had been hanging on the porch rail and said, "How about this?"

"Forget it." Jim said and led the way out to the kennel just as he had years ago.

As we approached the kennel, Jim called, "Come on out, Sarah. I want you to meet some young friends of mine."

And slowly out of her box and into the run came Sarah. She was one of the best looking, grey-muzzled old English setters I had ever seen. She stretched and blinked in the bright sun then carefully made her way to the gate where she sat down and looked steadily at Jim. Although she had a few thumps of her tail to acknowledge our pats, all of her loving attention was focused on Jim.

"Where did you find her?" I asked. "In a way we found each other," Jim said. "The dog warden was looking for somebody to take her, and he thought of me. It was probably the resemblance," Jim chuckled. "Had her a week now, and we get along fine. She's a good dog."

Grouse hunting season was soon with us again, and Bill asked Jim and his new/old dog to join us. After a long pause on the phone, he accepted. That morning, Jim insisted we leave him and Sarah to work out a hunt at their own pace. I watched them start along the sunny side of Poplar Ridge, and they both knew what they were doing—just a lot slower.

Along about 10 o'clock, we heard a single shot up on the ridge. When we came back to the wagon at noon, we found them both sound asleep in the back seat. Sarah's head was on Jim's lap, and a nice ruffed grouse was at his feet. As Bill and I looked at the tired, old pair of hunters, something must have stirred up my hay fever because my eyes watered, and I found it hard to speak. Bill had the same trouble and blamed it on the pollen. It was always bad that time of year.

28 A FOOT AT A TIME

WHETHER your gun rack carries only a few well-worn pieces or a full line of well-kept firearms, did you ever notice how the simple act of just picking up a certain gun often carries you back to a particular hunt somewhere in your past? For a short moment you seem to live it all again. Nothing new about this obvious observation, but I've also discovered that it can happen when you open your closet door and look at all those old hunting boots and shoes. Each pair seems to be waiting quietly for you to pull them on, lace them up and go hunting again.

Not long ago my wife suggested again that I . . . "sort out all of those old boots and shoes. Throw or give away the ones you'll never wear again and clean out that hunting closet before they raise our fire insurance rates." So one dark and gloomy winter day, with a lack of anything else to do, I finally started the task.

Frankly, I didn't get very far. I began my survey way back in the corner of the closet. The first pair of boots I dragged out into the light made me sit back on the floor and look them over. Big, black and fully caulked with 39 short metal spikes (I counted them) on each boot plus steel heel and toe plates. These hand-made Currins logger's boots weighed seven pounds on the bathroom scale. That's why an old-time lumberjack's threat "to put the boots to you" was nothing to ignore. Three and a half pounds on each foot. No wonder I haven't worn them lately. Lately? At least 34 years ago on the Olympic Peninsula in Washington was the last time.

World War II was over, and I was still attached to the Naval

THE BACK PAGE

Auxiliary Air Station at Quillayute, Washington. It was a lonely and remote air base often described as "the place where the mountain lions carry umbrellas." Only 130 inches of rain per year—that's over 10 feet. Rain forest. Olympic elk hunting. Almost up to the tops of these 13-inch boots in heavy, wet, green moss which thickly covered the ground and the gigantic fir trees as well.

My shipmate, a Missouri squirrel hunter named Andy Neal, and I were wandering around in those big, rainy woods near Forks, Washington, when we had our chance at a bull elk. I was carrying my Remington Model 8 autoloading rifle in .35 Rem. caliber, and it did the job with one lucky shot at about 100 yards. It was my first elk, and evidently the first one Andy had ever seen because he whistled softly and said, "Lot bigger than a squirrel, isn't he?" when we walked up to where the animal lay.

Up to now we had looked like old hands at the game. However, when my trusty, stag-handled, clasp knife which had served me well on deer bounced off that tough elk hide as if I had tried to stab a steel radial truck tire, I knew we were in trouble. Somehow we had to get that elk skinned, quartered and moved out to our pickup truck parked out on the logging road a good mile away. So, mustering all our woodcraft skills and lore of the forest, we went back to town for help.

Fortunately, we found Bill Corrigan at home, and after listening to our story with some amusement he kindly consented to go back with us and give us a hand with the right knife, a small Swede saw and three packboards almost the size of kitchen tabletops. These caulked boots then served me well as I staggered out of the woods with a full packboard up and over the fallen moss-covered logs and back to the truck. Two round trips and I never slipped once, but I did have a little trouble getting up into the cab of the truck. Very high step. I *know* my wife would want me to keep these boots. What's more, I could possibly wear them when I'm cutting the grass. The caulks would aerate the lawn. So back they go in the closet.

What about these old jodhpur boots of unfinished cowhide? I can still read "Made in Kenya" on the inside of these comfortable old friends. I am certainly no Peter Hathaway Capstick, and there's no blood from killing a charging rhino at 10 paces on these boots, but just handling them takes me back to my one and only trip to the glories of East Africa. My eye goes directly to the bookshelf near the closet and my dog-eared copy of that great hunting story, *The Green Hills of Africa* by Ernest Hemingway. I am about to get up and reach for it when the sound of my wife's voice comes up the stairs.

"I don't hear much fuss up there. How are you coming with that closet?"

I mumble something in reply, then these boots take me back to the Baja in Mexico, hunting white-winged doves with Joe Foss at a desert waterhole near the Rancho Buena Vista. We were making one of the TV movie series, "Joe Foss, Outdoorsman," and I was fortunate enough to be Joe's hunting partner. Good thing that Bob Halmi's camera didn't come in closer to me when the doves began to fly. They came by the thousands, and in my scramble for shells, I tried twice to load my package of Rolaids in the gun. I wouldn't say I was overly excited, but I wasn't quite as calm, cool and collected as I might have been. What a shoot to remember—and back go the boots in the closet.

Look at these Vasque mountain boots. Well-worn but still in good shape. I definitely remember them with the greatest affection and satisfaction—and I also remember where I got them. It was from "Ole" Olsen of Red Wing shoes. I was about to go to Nepal on a trip I can only describe as "Aging office worker tackles high Himalayas." Ole kindly offered to help me pick out the right kind of boots because if your feet give out somewhere up there on the roof of the world you are in serious trouble. You can't just call a cab. Everything moves by foot. Ankle-high, rough-finished and with Vibram soles, these grand old boots never pinched me, never rubbed me wrong all the way from Kathmandu to the Tibetan border and back. I huffed and puffed up to 14,500 feet without a slip and then down from Langtang with my toes feeling like they were coming out through the front of the boots. But no blisters for me. When I asked our leader, Dr. Bob Fleming, how far we had walked, he said, "On a straight line and without the ups and downs, it was 98 miles. But you can claim a hundred miles, Jack. You staggered a lot!"

All this was interrupted by a call of "lunch is ready." I put the Vasque boots gently back and shut the door. Somehow I never have gotten back to cleaning out that closet.

29 THE FOUR WORST SHOTS I EVER MADE

"T HE Five Most Often Traded Professional Baseball Players," or "Twelve Possible Sites for the Garden of Eden." These are from *The Book of Lists,* a current paperback bestseller. Full of unusual "lists," you can find out the "Ten Most Difficult Mothers-in-Law" in history or "16 Notable Persons Struck By Lightning." A completely unimportant book, but it's fun to read. I recommend it.

Being easily swayed by major developments in trivia, I set out immediately upon completion of this book to make my own "lists." My first attempt was "The 10 Best Shots I Ever Made." Lord knows I've made a lot of shots in my lifetime, but try as I would I couldn't come up with that many good ones. So I switched to "The 10 Worst Shots I Ever Made." That was easier but so damaging to what little self-confidence I still have— carried over from the ignorance of my youth—that I cut the list down to "The Four Worst Shots I Ever Made."

First Shot: I was whitetail hunting in the late 30's on the Gunflint Trail in northern Minnesota. We were hunting out of Don Gapen's camp on Hungry Jack Lake. (You fly fishermen probably know that Don Gapen invented the famous muddler minnow, which has nothing at all to do with this story.) There was new snow, and I was on a stand while my dad and Don made a short drive. I was armed with a newly-introduced Remington Model 81 autoloader in .35 caliber borrowed from my dad's gun samples. Since I was fresh from a fall of pheasant hunting in South Dakota, the new shotgun-style stock felt just right to me as I snapped the rifle to my shoulder several times

95

in practice and waited quietly for a big buck. And *big* he was, coming across a clearing at full speed no further than 40 yards away. I know that all you deer hunters have seen the biggest buck on the North American continent—several times. But this buck was bigger than that. With a set of horns that a flock of crows could roost in and a neck thicker than a Guernsey bull's, you wondered how he could get through the woods without knocking down the trees. The rifle came to my shoulder, just like a shotgun, while I lined up the iron sights and swung smoothly *ahead* of the running deer with a lead of about three feet—just right for a crossing South Dakota pheasant. Four shots . . . and I never touched him. When my dad came along on the drive and asked "Where is he?" all I could say, with my head down, was, "I *led* him like a rooster."

Second Shot: (Excuse me while I dry my tears from the last one.) This sad story has to do with the ruffed grouse, one of the most sought after birds in the Connecticut woods. A plump fantail in hand is a genuine trophy in these parts and hard to come by. It had been a long, dry morning on Den Road with my young friend, Bill Coleman, and Bones, my Brittany spaniel.

Somehow on the way back to the car I wandered down a trail off the old woods road and found myself on the edge of a marsh. I stood there for a moment looking sadly out over the bog with my 20-gauge autoloader in hand. Then it happened. With a thundering whir of wings, not *one* but *three* grouse got up at my feet—a perfect left angle, a straightaway and an easy right angle. Doubles on grouse are feats of a lifetime, but here was a possible triple. With cat-like speed I pulled down on the left hand bird—and pulled—and pulled—and pulled. Empty gun. I had failed to load after lunch.

Third Shot: (I'll wait while you put away your handkerchief.) Before I start this one, why is it that most pheasant hunting pictures show the bird flushing at the hunter's feet? How about that running cock bird that flushes just out of range? Now I realize that doesn't make a good picture, especially if it shows the hunter shaking his fist at the fast-departing bird. Running pheasants—pen raised or not—can be a challenge. And that's why Alex Stott and I learned to stay with the dog at the Saugatuck Fish & Game Club, or we didn't get a shot.

Alex's black Lab, Mike, had the nose of a bloodhound and the endurance of a timber wolf on a running pheasant. He finally got them up—and you'd better be there when he did. Lulled into a false sense of security by a good day on pheasants

THE FOUR WORST SHOTS I EVER MADE

in the woods with Alex and Mike, I unwisely suggested that we swap our 12-gauge guns for smaller and more sporting arms.
"How about 28-gauge?" Alex asked.
"Okay," I said.
So next time out, we both had our 28-gauge autoloaders. As luck would have it, though, that day the birds were *runners*. All pheasants will run, but these birds seemed to have been crossed with jackrabbits. The birds ran wild, and so did Mike with nose to ground, in and out of brush piles, hell for leather, over and under stone walls, through the briars and finally a far-off "cackling" flush. Alex and I ran too, as much as we could to keep up with Mike. Our shots were long ones, and the 28-gauge load brought down no birds. Finally, exhausted and about to give up, we heard Mike bark "treed." We found him looking up, with an occasional eager bark at a big cock pheasant perched in the top of a tall but thin maple tree.
"Okay," said Alex, "I'll shake him out. Get ready."
So I did, and at the first shake the pheasant, with complete disdain, fully decorated the top of my new hunting cap. While Alex clung to the tree with laughter, the bird took off. I shot twice. Alex recovered and shot once. The bird sailed away down the hill with Mike after him. When he finally came back empty-mouthed to the tree, where we waited, he seemed to avoid a direct look at either of us. He actually acted embarrassed.
Fourth Shot: Over the years it has been my privilege to have hunted with some famous outdoor writers and editors, like the late Jack O'Connor, Charlie Askins, Jim Carmichel, Bob Brister, Elmer Keith, and George Martin. Although I certainly won no medals, I usually managed to stay in there fairly well with these experts. That is, until a goose hunting day in Maryland when my partner was Grits Gresham, well-known writer, TV personality, all-around nice guy and an excellent shot. That day, to my chagrin, I couldn't have hit a Canada goose if it had waddled into the blind and pecked at my rubber boots. Finally, after a particularly abysmal and fruitless shot on my part, Grits said kindly, "It's a mighty tricky wind."
Which reminds me of Henry Davis' story of the Georgia quail guide standing behind a client who, in spite of countless covey rises, had yet to hit a bird with his double gun. After another pair of misses, the guide finally said, "Colonel, that gun of yours ejects shells further backward than any gun I ever seed."

THE DOG NEXT DOOR '30

I
T was Christmas morning when Billy Cochrane, the kid
next door, rang our door bell and stood there holding the biggest, blackest and roundest Labrador retriever pup I had ever
seen. He was a full arm-load—all legs, fat belly, huge feet and
a red tongue to lick Billy's shining face.

"He's mine," Billy said excitedly. "We just got him and I
picked him out. His name is Sam, and he's the biggest one in
the litter."

"Just great, Billy, and if he grows up to match his feet you'll
need a horse trailer to haul him up to the River Blind."

"And Dad says I can train him myself. I've got a book and
a retrieving dummy, and I'll work with him every day. I told
Dad he's going to be the best dog on the whole river."

Then I saw Nipper, their little cocker spaniel, come through
the hedge. He stopped short when he saw us and turned back
into his own yard.

"What does Nipper think of him?" I asked.

"He bit him. Nipper doesn't seem to like him very much."

Like all the months I remember on Elm Street, they went by
too fast. I could hardly believe that it was hunting season again.

I couldn't make it on opening day, and I was anxious to hear
how big Sam made out on his first duck hunt. But there was no
report from next door until I met John Cochrane, Billy's father,
at the mailbox.

"How did you make out last Saturday, John?" I asked.

"We didn't. That big dog of Billy's is gun-shy."

"That's a shame. Did he retrieve anything?"

"He certainly did. Retrieved most of our *decoys*. No sooner did we pitch them out in the river than he brought them back. All tangled up. Couldn't stop him. Never saw anything like it. Finally had to wallop him with a paddle. Then when we started to shoot, he got under the bench in the blind and wouldn't come out."

"That's too bad. How did Billy take all this?"

"Oh, full of excuses for his dog. Tears in his eyes, I'm afraid. Just sat there and tried to pat Sam under the bench. But he's got to face up to it. We've got a big, gun-shy, one hundred pound Lab on our hands. Eats like a horse and retrieves everything but ducks. He's got to go."

No more from next door until John invited me to join them in their river blind on the coming Saturday. Billy and his dog were going to be there, too.

Saturday dawned as a good duck day—winds strong in the northwest with grey clouds racing across a cold, pale sunrise. The decoys were out front and working well in the dark river current. John, Billy, Sam and I were snug in the river blind with the skiff "grassed up" and hidden in the mouth of the creek a hundred yards or more above us. Billy kept his hand on Sam who watched the bobbing decoys in the river and whined at every stick that drifted by. There was a look of such eager hope on the boy's face that I found it hard to look at him.

How he found us I don't know, but suddenly Nipper was in the blind. Duck hunting wasn't his assignment, and he had been left at home, but he had evidently followed us up the river, and there he was, with wiggles of greeting for us, and a few growls for Sam. John threatened to beat him with a stick about the size of a soda straw. Nipper knew he didn't mean it, and he was soon sitting beside John, all ears and attention.

It was a high and wide shot out over the river. Maybe too high, but John took it anyway, and down came a big drake mallard, stone dead and belly up, at least 75 yards out in the fast current. At the sound of the shot, Sam went under the bench and then suddenly, with an excited "yip," Nipper was gone—scrambling down over the bank and into the big river. John blasted on his whistle, but Nipper kept on swimming with his eye on that duck. And then the white water of the main current caught him and to our horror, Nipper was being swept away by the fast water.

Stunned silence until a white-faced Billy screamed, "Fetch, 99

Sam, fetch," and out from under the bench like a black bear out of his den came Sam. He stopped, saw Nipper, and with a leap off the bank, hit the water with a mighty splash and was underway at full steam. How that dog could swim! Angling down and across the river, we soon saw the heads of the two dogs together. And they stayed together, because the big Labrador had Nipper by the collar.

They made shore on the long sand bar a quarter of a mile below us. John and Billy waded out over their boottops to reach them. John picked up Nipper and put him on the beach where he began to cough up river water, stopped to shake himself, fell over, got up and shook once more. Then the little wet dog stood for a moment with his head down, staggered over to Sam and tried to bite him. John snatched him up again, held him tight and turned his back on us. I think that the stern Mr. Cochrane was about to cry. Finally he found his red bandana, blew his nose loudly and put Nipper back on his feet.

Then John turned to Sam, whose tail was going full tilt, gently patted his big wet head and said quietly, while Billy grinned, "Come on Sam, you big ox. Let's go home."

I'd like to report that Sam has finally added ducks to the list of items he readily retrieves, but up to now he hasn't. But I can tell you one thing. There is no more talk next door about getting rid of Sam.

31 A CHRISTMAS HUNT

WHENEVER I hear "Jingle Bells" this time of the year, I often wonder how many of us have ever really known "what fun it is to ride in a one-horse open sleigh" or actually remember "chestnuts roasting by an open fire." In these times, our Christmas is more likely to be a ride on the new snow tires to McDonalds and a package of organic peanuts in the microwave oven.

It's easy for some of us older birds to be sad about collapsible and reusable plastic Christmas trees and interstellar space games for the kids that launch a computerized attack on Mars. What ever happened to wooden "Tinker Toys" and "Lincoln Logs"? But while we may regret many of the modernized and synthetic changes in this holiday, there is one aspect of Christmas-giving for every last hunter that always remains the same.

You've probably guessed it. It's that carefully wrapped, long, flat and rectangular package that seems to glow all by itself as it waits beneath the Christmas tree. And when the package is eagerly opened by young and trembling hands, it's every one of us who looks up again at Dad and Mother and says in a choked voice, "Gee whiz! It's a *real* gun."

My first gun was a single-barrel, single-shot Iver-Johnson .410-gauge shotgun. I don't remember exactly how old I was, but the gun and I were about the same length. No sooner was the gun out of the box than my Dad started the safety lessons. "Watch that muzzle!" He showed me how to open the gun, load it with a dummy shell, close it and put the hammer on half-cock.

101

With two upset chairs to represent a fence, I learned to open my gun, take out the shell and climb through or over the barrier. I was greatly impressed by my Dad's story of his first hunt as a youngster with Granddad when he forgot to open and unload his brand new gun before climbing through a fence. Granddad then told him quietly that since he evidently wasn't going to be a safe hunter he had no right to own a gun at all and to just put it on the ground and leave it there. The hunt continued for some time with Dad straggling along and looking back sadly at his gun while fighting back the tears. I can imagine his desolation.

Finally Granddad stopped and said "If you are ready now to handle that gun safely, you'd better go back and get it."

Dad said his feet barely touched the ground as he raced back to the fence and his gun. Imagining him trudging back to the group with gun on shoulder, I can almost see his broad grin. He was now ready to hunt safely.

My little Iver-Johnson was a good one, and it started both me and my younger brother, Bob, on the way to becoming hunters. My first real hunt with my new gun didn't happen until I had carried the .410 all fall with just that everlasting dummy shell in the chamber—no live ammo. I tagged along with my Dad after grouse, woodcock, jacksnipe and rabbits and made some spectacular "silent" shots on all kinds of game. Then came the day when I was allowed to empty a box of three-inch .410 shells in my hunting coat pocket. What a wonderful feeling. The coat was a little too big for me, and I had to put my hand and arm down pretty far into the pocket to reach those shells. Just to pat them and know that they were there felt great.

Looking back now, it was hardly an ordinary Wisconsin rabbit hunt we had that Christmas week when I was carrying real ammo. First of all, our host for the hunt was my Dad's good friend, Jack McBride, a well-known Milwaukee sportsman who had been a professional rollerskater, bowler, shooter and restaurant owner. One of the friendliest men I ever met, this smiling little Irishman was a great and popular figure.

When we picked up Mr. McBride, he came out of his house, stopped and went back in, finally to emerge with a straw hamper of pre-Prohibition champagne. He had suddenly remembered it was his birthday.

What a bright, shining, snow-covered day it was out there on Mr. McBride's farm. The little beagles were noisy, yapping and tugging at their leashes. All except "Schnappsey," usually the best hound in the pack. He just sat there looking sad and being quiet.

"Look at that Schnappsey hound," Jack said. "As soon as there's snow on the ground, he shuts up. A silent tracker. Not a sound out of him even when he's driving hard."

"Why does he do that?" I asked seriously.

"If I only knew," Jack grinned, "I'd call him into the house and talk to him. Maybe his feet are cold, and we should knit him two pairs of socks."

I missed the first two bouncing cottontails I shot at but rolled the third one. There were grilled Milwaukee bratwurst sausage sandwiches for lunch with watercress from the ice-rimmed spring brook where the champagne bottles were cooling.

At the end of the day, the champagne corks were popped. There were elegant toasts made to Jack's birthday and a small one—one sip only from Dad's glass—made to me and my first rabbit. We didn't go home in a one-horse open sleigh, but I can remember sleepily watching the Christmas moon sparkling on the snow as Dad drove the old Essex carefully back to town.

32 A BUG ON A STRING

MOST dogs in our country town are hunting dogs. So it wasn't so much the bride Bill Kane, my duck-hunting partner, brought home from the city that dumfounded everyone. It was his bride's dog—an outrageous, miniature, black French poodle named Jacques. Not only city-born, but city-bred and pampered as an only child.

When he and Jean parked downtown on their first shopping trip, passers-by stopped in their tracks at the sight of Jacques sitting up in the front seat—rhinestone collar sparkling, red-ribbon bow topping off his pom-pom. He returned their stares and gibes with perfect aplomb and twitched his aristocratic whiskers in fastidious disdain.

In the back seat, with an affable grin for everybody, slouched old Mike, Bill's black Labrador, one of the best retrievers on the river. I stopped and gave him a pat.

"Hey, Mike, who's your pal in the front seat?"

I could have sworn I heard him say, "Ain't he somethin', now?"

It was a hot summer afternoon when my wife and I called on Bill and Jean. Seeing them together, you knew all was well. Bill had acquired a wonderful wife *and* a nifty little dude of a French poodle.

As I opened the door to leave, a big gray squirrel scampered toward the oak by the driveway. Jacques crossed the yard in a flash of rhinestones. The squirrel, of course, beat him to it. On his way back to the porch, he touched noses with Mike.

105

THE BACK PAGE

"Guess I'll have to fill you in on squirrels," Mike must have said.

Jean was aghast: "But what if he'd caught it?"

"Don't worry, dear. Jacques' poodle ancestors were French hunting dogs. They still call it 'chien canard'—duck dog. His fancy grooming is a throwback to the custom of clipping their long coats to make them better water dogs."

"Now you tell me," Jean said.

"It never came up before. Jacques is really a hunter at heart —pom-pom, red bow and all."

Jean sighed. "Well, I certainly hope it doesn't ruin him, or anything . . ." Bill just smiled.

The town was ready to forget all about Jacques until that rainy Saturday when owner and dog walked by Meyer's Barber Shop. Jean was decked out in a stylish yellow slicker and rain hat. So was Jacques. A smartly tilted sou'wester slanted off his pom-pom. Besides that, he wore a tailored yellow slicker to match and, so help me, a set of little yellow boots. He strained the leash tight, picking out puddles to splash through, just like a kid.

As luck would have it, Bill and I were waiting for monthly haircuts and discussing plans for the first day of duck season. Paul Bascom, a Saturday-morning regular, spotted them first. "Look at that!" he whooped. "A bug on a string, wearing rubber boots."

Bill came out of his chair, red to the ears. "That bug on a string," he said coldly, "is my wife's French poodle. He's got as much hunt in him as any dog you ever owned."

Jean and Jacques turned the corner. Paul said apologetically, "No offense, Bill. I wouldn't know about his hunting. I just wouldn't know."

Bill got his hat and coat. He left without a word—and without his haircut.

I picked up Bill before sun-up on opening day. He was waiting for me with *two* black dogs: big Mike and little Jacques. No rhinestones, no red ribbon, just a plain leather collar. Bill climbed into the car.

"Hope you don't mind. I've just got to find out about Jacques. Jean went to the city yesterday. He's big enough to retrieve a teal—I think."

The wind was just right for the high-bank blind. The minute we got set, the blue-winged teal began to move. On the first bird down, Mike hit the water with a splash. His retrieve was perfect. Jacques didn't flinch at the gun. He just sat there and shook! Fear? Cold? Some wild inner drive he couldn't understand? Who knows? Maybe all three.

The second flight yielded a double. When Mike broke for his retrieve, damned if he didn't shove Jacques with his nose and give a "woof" that clearly said, "C'mon, partner, let's get to work."

A half-inch rope couldn't have held Jacques back. He plunged over the side and swam for the drake greenwing like a black muskrat. He found the bird and started back. It was a struggle, but he kept coming for all he was worth, eyes popping, bedraggled pom-pom down around his ears somewhere. But he had his duck. Mike was already back with his bird, and he and Bill were barking and yelling at Jacques, so excited they almost fell out of the blind.

I never heard exactly what happened when Bill arrived home with Jacques. It couldn't have been too bad, because on Christmas Eve at the Kanes, Jacques, groomed to the ears, greeted us at the door. At his side, wig-wagging "Merry Christmas" with his tail, was his hunting partner, Mike. That big black Lab sure looked funny with a splashy red silk bow tied to his collar. If it wasn't for that foolish, happy, "Look-what-I-got" grin of his, you'd think he'd been wearing one all his life.

THE
DEAF
DEER 33

formal New Year's resolution can be a fearsome thing. Properly couched in firm and unrelenting language, a hard-nosed resolution can be absolutely airtight and escapeproof. He who accepts such a resolution to improve his conduct and moral fiber rarely finds a way out during the year. He either holds to the firm resolve or fails miserably—twisting and turning on the point of his own conscience.

That is why I have devised a new and more friendly form of New Year's resolutions. I call it my list of "I'm certainly going to try to" resolutions. Here is how it works.

Some time between Christmas and New Year's Day you carefully write down all the things you believe could be improved by your own actions in the coming year. If you really try, it gets to be quite a list. To shorten it to a workable size, you immediately strike out hopeless tasks like "lose 30 pounds by Lincoln's Birthday" or "be more cheerful with a smile for everybody before you have your morning coffee." One of the first items I always remove is "clean my garage by building a wall tool rack, like my neighbor, that has a definite and designated place for every single indoor and outdoor tool I own." I really don't have that many tools—at least I don't think I do. I've never had them all in one place long enough to count them.

It is often necessary to separate the resolutions into certain classifications of activity. This year I ended up with quite a few items listed under—of all things—hunting.

Here are a few of them:

As a hunter, I'm certainly going to try to (1) "Follow a physical-fitness program well before opening day so I won't disappoint my dog by sitting down so often that he wears himself out coming back to see where I am." (2) "Exercise my dog enough so that when he comes back to see where I am he doesn't just sit down with me—and pant." (3) "Take the gun that isn't working right to the gunsmith today and not just before the season." A gunsmith friend of mine told me that when he once told an impatient hunter, who wanted an on-the-spot repair, that he couldn't have his gun ready until the next day: "Tomorrow!" the hunter objected. "If I had wanted it *tomorrow*, I would have brought it in *tomorrow.*" No wonder gunsmiths are grumpy characters.

(4) "After I get my shotgun fixed, I will try to sharpen up my shooting eye on some flying clay targets, either with some of my friends and a hand trap or at the local gun club." There was a time when the average hunter showed up at the local skeet or trap club only to find, as a friend of mine said, "a bunch of sharpshooters running around with signs on their shooting jackets like 'Interplanetary 410 Skeet Champion' and 'modest' little long-run patches like 100 and 200 straight. I was about to sneak back to my car but then decided to try it. Got a snappy 6 out of 25—unaided. Before I got back in the clubhouse, there was my lousy score and name on the big scoreboard. Never again." But I'm glad to report that those times have changed. Gun clubs realize your importance, and you will now receive a warm welcome. Personal instruction, too, if you want it. Give them a ring or just go out with one of the shooters.

(5) "Start right now to get in some range practice with my deer rifle. Make sure it's sighted-in correctly, and that I can hit what I shoot at." After deer season last year, an irate customer came into our local gun shop with the rifle he had just purchased from my friend Steve. "There was the biggest buck I ever saw feeding in the meadow. Not more than a hundred yards," he said. "I shot at him three times with this rifle, and he *never even looked up.* Finally, he just trotted off into the brush. How do you explain that?"

"Probably a deaf deer," Steve said.

Further questioning, of course, revealed that the customer had not sighted-in his rifle because, as he said "It was brand new. Aren't they sighted-in at the factory?"

"Yes," Steve answered, "but never hunt with a rifle that you haven't checked out on a target." Okay, Steve. I hear you talking.

(6) "Make an honest effort to take a youngster hunting. It's

about time I pass along to a new generation what safe and sane hunting is all about and, by my example, show some young hunter—boy or girl—that hunting is never measured by the size of the bag alone.

These are brave words, but I fully intend to carry them out. A lot of us are concerned these days about a few "win-oriented" hunters who seem to forget all of their indoor manners when they go outdoors. Their deplorable actions in running up a winning score of "game in the pocket and meat in the freezer" embarrasses us all. So how do we stop it? We make sure that every young hunter coming into the sport gets off to the right start through hunter education courses and guys like you and me teaching them the way.

So these are just a few of my "certainly going to try to" friendly resolutions for hunting in 1980. 1980? Great balls of fire! What has become of all those years? I think I'll go and lie down for a while.

34 IS BIGFOOT STILL ROAMING THE WOODS?

THE two wilderness campers were sound asleep in their snug down bags and tightly zippered nylon tent when they were suddenly awakened by heavy footfalls cracking brush at the door of their tent. Wide-eyed and sitting up straight in their sleeping, bags one camper whispered to his partner, "What's that?"

"Don't know," he whispered back. "Take a look. You've got the flashlight."

"I'd rather not," was the answer.

"Then give me the light. I'll do it."

Slowly unzipping the tent flap with a trembling hand, the brave camper shot a shaft of light out into the darkness. Then quickly closing the zipper, he snapped off the light and fell back onto his bed with a sigh of relief.

"Thank God," he said. "It's only a grizzly bear. I thought it was *Bigfoot*!"

This probably never happened, but with all the hunters' talk I've been hearing lately around campfires and hot stoves it probably could. It certainly looks like old Sasquatch, or Bigfoot, has taken to roaming the woods again and has got a lot of folks scared stiff. In fact, I just got a letter from my friend, Ron Liebler, who reports, "We have had some very strange happenings around Yale during the last few months." Ron, who is a hunter and a taxidermist, lives on a farm near the small town of Yale, Michigan, up in the Thumb area of the Wolverine State. (The other Yale, as you know, is in Connecticut and   111 regularly beats Harvard.) The newspaper clippings Ron sent report several sightings on the Barone farm of a large creature which walks on two legs, is at least seven feet high, and has a 15-inch footprint. A neighbor, Leland Shepherd, reported that something had ripped open a tent, damaged two barn doors, and pushed in a pig pen fence. On November 20, one of the Barones' daughters, 13-year-old Tina "accidentally touched something furry in the barn." It is also reported that absolutely no sightings of Tina have been made in the vicinity of that barn since. For which no one blames her a bit.

How will you be able to recognize a Bigfoot if you happen to see one in the woods? I'm glad you asked. Based on my haphazard research and previous reports, Bigfoot ranges from six to 10 feet tall, and more than 60 percent of the observers reported a height of seven to eight feet. I don't suppose it would stand still for your tape measure, so if you can, take a good look at its feet. They are from 12 to 22 inches long, the most common being about 16 inches long and seven inches wide at the ball of the foot. Bigfoot walks erect on these big feet and with very human leg and arm movements. (I failed to find any information on how fast Bigfoot can walk. This is important to me because if I ever see one I would like to plan just how fast I will have to walk in the *opposite* direction.)

So that you won't possibly mistake Bigfoot for your partner or a fellow hunter, here is another tip. The creature is covered with long black or brown hair, except around the eyes, palms of his hands, and the soles of its huge feet. For more positive identification you could probably ask it to hold up its feet. If the soles are bare, you could reciprocate by showing it the bottom of *your* feet as you rapidly disappear over the hill.

I really don't know why I seem to be kidding about Bigfoot because I have a very strong hunch that he really exists. A hard-bitten and down-to-earth explorer named David Thompson was one of the first white men ever to reach the Pacific Northwest back in 1811. And it was Thompson, who while crossing the Canadian Rockies, reported finding large animal tracks that were 14 inches long and eight inches wide—and *not* those of a bear. Since then there have been literally thousands of reports that describe some type of man-like ape creature that is huge, hairy, elusive, foul-smelling, capable of seeing in the dark, and roaming the back woods of North America.

I have never seen a Bigfoot, but I am convinced that I once came very close to meeting his cousin, the Abominable Snow-

112

man, who wanders in and out of the high valleys of the Himalayas. The Snowman, or Yeti as he is known in Nepal, is usually seen at night or at dusk and rarely below an altitude of 13,000 feet. And that's what it was, sundown and approaching a Nepalese high camp at above 14,000 feet. Following closely behind our pack-laden Tamang porters, we were moving slowly along a narrow mountain trail. Suddenly there was something unseen above us moving in the loose rocks that sent a few small stones flying out over our heads and down into the deep chasm yawning below us. The tired porters stopped and looked silently up the dark mountainside. "Yeti!" someone called, perhaps in jest; but the pace of the party noticeably quickened. In fact, my pace quickened so noticeably that I was one of the first to reach camp.

Superstitions usually retreat before the force of logic, but Bigfoot and his kind seem to persist. My predicament is somewhat akin to that of my friend, Noel Kelly of Balleyshannon, Ireland. Years ago and after a particularly unlucky day of "rough shooting" in the Galway marshes, we came in with one skinny jacksnipe apiece. Later on in the pub where we went to console each other and plan the next day's hunt, Noel said, "When that black cat crossed my path on the way to pick you up this morning, I should have gone home and got back in bed. But it's only a silly superstition, I said to myself."

"So it is," I agreed. "But we have many of your Irish superstitions, too, in the States. Like Friday the 13th?"

"A *very* bad day," Noel laughed.

"And walking under a ladder," I said.

"Oh no. Never do that," and he laughed again. "And never, never open an umbrella in the house."

"All pretty silly." "But you have one here in Ireland, that we don't have," I said.

"What's that?" Noel asked, still grinning.

"Well, you have the leprechauns. The ones you call "The Little People."

There was a long silence after that while Noel stared straight ahead. Finally he turned to me with a solemn face and said quietly, "Oh, you mean *them.*"

And right now that's how I feel about Bigfoot.

35 THE BIG TEN MAG

I don't usually go around introducing old guns to my friends but here is a gun I want you to meet. This was my Dad's gun. It's a Parker, 10-gauge magnum, double-barreled shotgun, chambered for 3½-inch shells with 32-inch barrels—choked full and full.

Let me check the chambers. O.K. Closes with a nice ring, doesn't it? Still good and tight. Here, try it to your shoulder. Oops! Don't drop it. Yes, it *is* a little heavy. About 11 pounds. And after you've lugged it along with a sack of decoys for more than ten minutes, it weighs just over 35 pounds! Why so heavy? Because it's designed to handle the most powerful shotgun shell on the market today. Here's one of them. It's 3½ inches long, loaded with five drams equivalent of smokeless powder and two ounces of shot. It's the 10-gauge magnum shell. Each round weighs about three ounces—six to a pound—or about 4½ pounds per box. So, if you're walking out to the blind with this gun and two boxes of shells, you're carrying 20 pounds. Heavily armed is right.

Does it kick? Well, it all depends on your ability to roll with the punch—like an old boxer. At least that's what I was told when I tried it for the first time, years ago, on a high flock of shovelers. How high? Well over 60 yards, and if you think that's not a long shot, just try pacing it off sometime. Hang your hat up on the mark, go back where you started and look at it. Now, where was I? Oh, yes, the shovelers, or spoonbills, we called them. A big bunch. So I swung well out ahead and tried the first barrel. With a "whomp!" it *rained* ducks. Three came down—stone dead. I vaguely remember firing the second barrel

115

somewhere in the general direction of the flock because the first shot had just about crossed my eyes. Three ducks? Yes. Three. But, remember, they were spoonbills, and it was said that you could bring down spoonbills by popping a paper bag when they flew over. Well, not really, but they were pretty easy to nail. But not so easy on my end of the gun. A real bump! I guess I didn't roll with the punch. And I never did really learn how to do it.

My dad, on the other hand, could stand up there on Hitke Pass in South Dakota with this gun and take a limit of high-flying ducks—65 to 75 yards—without a flinch. He had mastered not only the horizontal lead but also how high to hold over the target to compensate for the drop of the big charge of shot at long ranges. This gun got to be quite famous on those Dakota duck passes. What about geese? Seems hard to realize, but back in the 30s, there were very few geese of any kind on that flyway. Now they are there by the hundreds of thousands, thanks to good management.

And then there was the time down on the Illinois River when Paul Stroud, his black Lab retriever and I, armed with the big ten, were standing quietly in a small patch of dry, unpicked, standing corn. We were waiting for mallards to swing up off the river bottom and hopefully come over us. High shots, and hence the 10-guage mag, loaded with two ounces—a good solid hand-ful of #4 shot. It was quiet, standing there in the November sun, and no birds were moving. Suddenly, the Lab, bored with the waiting, went into business for himself and took out after a cottontail rabbit with a bark for every bounce as they both rattled back and forth through the standing corn. Paul's blasts on the whistle, until his eyes popped, were to no avail and the chase continued. Hardly a good setup for a wary mallard. I decided to give the Lab a hand and end all the ruckus. I raised the big gun and waited until the rabbit was a good 40 yards away and well out in front of the dog. "Ka-boom" the gun roared, and that charge of shot cut an unbelievable swath down through the dry corn with ears, stalks and leaves flying in every direction, and rolled the rabbit over without a wiggle. The Lab stopped dead in his tracks and looked back at me and the gun in some amazement, trotted over to the rabbit, picked it up and came back quietly to Paul's heel.

"What a gun," Paul laughed. "Now when the game warden shows up how are you going to explain that we haven't been scattering the corn to bait this field?"

I'll bet that Bill Harris, an old pro from Effingham, Illinois, well remembers the day he tried this gun on the pass at Blue Dog Lake near Waubay, South Dakota. I certainly do. Bill had lugged the big gun out on the pass, and while several of us were back at the station wagon, we heard what seemed like a pretty loud shot. Pretty soon Bill showed up, carrying the gun in both hands like he was returning a live snake he had unwisely borrowed. And in a loud voice (I can hear him now) Bill reported, "She *double-fired* on me—both barrels! Holy Golden! An overhead shot, and I know it compressed my ankle bones. Do I look any shorter? Holy Golden! Where's my own gun? If I'd been wearing rubber boots, I'd still be bouncing up and down out there. Gimme my own gun," he said and rummaged around in the back of the wagon, "and some reasonable shells too. I'll see you later. Holy Golden!" I remember how the sound of our laughs followed him down the meadow and out to the pass. Yes, I guess Bill Harris would tell you that it kicks a little.

Here, I'll put it back in the rack and thanks for listening to all this "I remember when" stuff.

Sure, I plan to shoot it again. Maybe down in Maryland, on the Eastern Shore. There's a world of geese there every fall. Say, that reminds me. Oh, you have to go? O.K. Well, stop by again any time.

EXACTLY HOW 36 IT HAPPENED

ONCE upon a time there was a young and strug-gling outdoor writer named Tom who wrote a lot of hunting and fishing stories. But, unfortunately, it seemed that his only readers were his loyal young wife, Elsie, who did the typing, and his Uncle Bill, who didn't have much else to do.

Regardless of how many times he sent off his carefully writ-ten, neatly typed hunting and fishing stories to the outdoor magazines, all he ever got back was a short, polite letter and a rejection slip. But Tom kept on trying.

One sunny day Elsie had just finished typing Tom's latest deer hunting story, so he walked downtown to pick up the family food stamps and mail off his new masterpiece to *Outdoor Universe*. Tom had just seen this magazine in the local library and had been impressed with an exciting, full-color series on "How to Hunt Marco Polo Sheep in Outer Mongolia with Your Wife" and a helpful, do-it-yourself article on "How to Update Your Old Electronic Fish-Finder with an Ice Pick."

As our hero passed his Uncle Bill's house, he saw him out in the backyard with a pump shotgun in his hand, staring up into the leafy branches of a big oak tree.

"Squirrel hunting, Uncle Bill?" Tom asked.

"Nope. Just looking for my magazine spring and three-shot plug," he answered.

"How'd they get up there?" Tom said.

"Forgot to put my thumb over the end of this danged maga-zine tube when I unscrewed the cap . . . and they just took off," he said, still looking up into the tree.

Tom, who knew a lot about the woods and nature since he was, after all, an outdoor writer, said, "Don't worry about it, Uncle Bill. Those leaves will thin out this fall, and you'll be able to see 'em in time for hunting season."

"Thanks, Tom," Uncle Bill said. "That's mighty straight thinking." And then seeing the big, brown manuscript envelope in Tom's hand, he asked, "Trying it again, boy?"

"Yes sir. But this one is a cinch to sell. It is all about our hunt last fall up on the Gunflint. Remember how I twisted my knee and stayed in camp and cooked that venison stew while the three of you drove all the way up to the Rose Lake burn . . . and I just hunted around camp with my bum knee. And I worked in all the details about my knee and just how you put that Ace bandage on it and the hot compresses the night before. And how the three of you had to roll out of bed long before daylight, and all that grumbling about who busted the mantle on the Coleman lamp, and the coffee that wouldn't boil, and how cold it was in the cabin. And then Charlie's old truck with the busted heater wouldn't start. And you guys had 45 miles yet to drive before you could hunt, and all I had to do was roll over in my nice warm bunk and go back to sleep."

"That's right," Uncle Bill said. "Exactly how it happened. And did you tell about fixing the venison stew and keeping the stove going so the stew could just simmer away all day long, and keeping the cabin nice and warm while you took it easy. And how you finally decided to take a look around camp on your own just for something to do."

"Exactly," Tom said. "I hobbled around out there for almost an hour and never saw hide nor hair of a deer, and then after dark you guys drove up with three nice bucks in the truck. And then, just because I had burned the stew a little on the bottom when the top came off the salt shaker and because I forgot to put in the onions, you guys all said it was the lousiest venison stew you had ever eaten. And my knee still hurts."

"That's exactly how it happened all right," Uncle Bill said. "Particularly the stew. Just plain awful." For a while he stood there staring at Tom and then he repeated, "That's exactly how it happened, all right. But somehow it doesn't sound like a 100 percent, genuine outdoor story. Aren't you supposed to have killed a big buck just back of the camp, and aren't we supposed to have come home completely skunked? And wasn't the stew supposed to be delicious?"

"But that isn't what happened," Tom protested.

THE BACK PAGE

"Sounds like the true story you were writing about Elsie and her first hunting trip. Didn't one of those outdoor magazines act interested?" Bill asked.

"You mean when Elsie went deer hunting with us. Just to see what it was all about."

"Don't seem to remember that. She get a shot?"

"Nope. All she got was lost. Left her stand to pick some bittersweet and wandered around for a few hours in Jackson Swamp. She got a small blister on her heel and a little frostbite on her nose. Guess I shouldn't have laughed when it got red and swelled up. Nothing to worry about, but she said if I ever invited her again, she'd wrap the rifle around my neck. And the magazine didn't seem to like my outline, so I never finished the story. All I wanted to do was tell it exactly how it happened."

"I know, I know," Uncle Bill said. "But isn't it a lot like that story you were writing about finding one of great granddad's homemade muskie plugs?"

"That's right. I did find one," said Tom. "Just as we were packing up to leave that expensive resort up at Muskie Bay. Been there a week, spent more than we should have, and hadn't raised a single muskie. Fished hard, from dawn to dark, too. And then there it was—way down in the bottom of my big tackle box—one of Great Granddad's special muskie plugs made out of a corncob and a whole squirrel skin and full of hooks. I had never used it before, but just on a hunch I snapped it on my rod, left Elsie with the packing, and went down to the dock for one last cast. I wound up and heaved that big old plug as far as I could, way out to the edge of the lily pads. It made a splash like a diving beaver, and then I began to crank it back . . . *slowly*. Looked just like a swimming squirrel." Tom stopped.

"Then what happened?" Uncle Bill said. "As if I didn't know."

"Nothing," Tom said. "So I just cranked it all the way in and went back to the cottage. That was the day we had two flat tires on the way home."

"Quite a story," Uncle Bill said.

So that's the way we leave Tom and Uncle Bill. Tom has yet to sell an outdoor story, but still he keeps on writing. And every one of them is "exactly how it happened."

37 RETURN OF THE FALCON

THE Brittany spaniel eagerly working the pheasant cover with a lot of wiggle suddenly comes to a hard point. The falconer "unhoods" the bird perched on his leather glove, and the large, dark, piercing eyes of the peregrine falcon flash in the sunlight as she is released. With powerful beats of her long, pointed wings, the falcon soon climbs to the proper "pitch" almost a hundred yards above the pointing Brittany. She circles there in a "waiting on" position. The falconer then moves in, flushing the big cock pheasant. The watching falcon high overhead slides off to one side, folds her wings, and begins her dive. "Stooping" to her prey, this feathered bullet of a bird has been timed at more than 200 miles per hour in this incredible dive. Shooting out her big, yellow, sharp-taloned feet, she strikes the pheasant in mid-air with such force that the feathers fly and the pheasant plummets to the earth. Circling down, the falcon lands on her prey with wide-spread wings, jabs down her notched beak, and quickly severs the spinal cord of the stunned bird. No sooner does the falcon fasten its talons to the pheasant than her hunting partner, the Brittany, arrives on the scene and retrieves, believe it or not, both birds—the pheasant and the attached falcon.

Hardly an ordinary pheasant hunting scene, this took place near Centerville, South Dakota, at a field trial of The North American Falconers Association. Dr. Heinz Meng, who told me all this, said the peregrine falcon in the story had been raised and trained prior to the federal Endangered Species Act of 1973. Dr. Meng, a biology professor at the State University of New York in New Paltz, is the first scientist ever to successfully and   121 consistently breed the peregrine in captivity and return the young to the wild. "Doc" Meng is an avid hunter and falconer —far from a dusty and pedantic professor—and is one of the world's foremost authorities on peregrines. He has a sense of humor, too. Patting his shiny pate, he said with a grin, "This is why I get along so well with the hawks. They think I'm a bald eagle."

No doubt, many of you know what havoc the recent and tragic mistake of using DDT and similar deadly and enduring pesticides caused among all wildlife. But it takes "Doc" Meng really to impress you with what these pesticides did to his beloved birds of prey.

"We were unable to find a single nesting pair of peregrines anywhere in the eastern United States," he states. "The American peregrine was the first bird conclusively shown to have been killed by pesticides."

This and other examples of wildlife destruction finally led to an almost complete ban on DDT by the federal government in 1970. The sad part, of course, is that this protection came too late to save the peregrine in the wild.

"Will they ever live and breed here again?" I asked.

"Yes," Dr. Meng answered. "Many of us believe they can be brought back."

Led by Dr. Meng's example, scientists are now breeding peregrines in captivity and attempting to restock the species in the United States as the lingering pesticide residues diminish with the passage of time. If you would like to read the fascinating story of how the falcon is being brought back from the brink of extinction, send for *Falcons Return,* an excellent and profusely illustrated hard-cover book. This authoritative and exciting report on the peregrine project and the ancient sport of falconry (where, incidentally, the red-tailed hawk is the most popular bird used today) is available for $8.00 postpaid from The Peregrine Falcon Foundation, Dept. AH, 10 Joalyn Road, New Paltz, N.Y. 12561. This is Dr. Meng's enterprise, and any tax-deductible contributions to the Foundation, which are urgently needed to continue this good work, will be greatly appreciated.

When Dr. Meng, who recently spent the night at our house during one of his fund-raising lecture tours, found out that I was planning to write this story for *American Hunter,* he fixed me with a hard look and said, "From one hunter to another, will you *please* ask your readers to help spread the word on stopping the illegal and tragic practice of shooting hawks, owls . . . and even eagles? Fortunately for all of us, there are only a few so-called "hunters" still guilty of this disgraceful conduct. And I believe that their reason for breaking the federal and state laws in this manner is sheer ignorance. I refuse to call them hunters, but that's what the press calls them. And we who hunt legitimately suffer for their mindless and ignorant acts," Dr. Meng said with more than a little fervor.

"I'm certainly not apologizing for these trigger-happy guys, but don't you think that many of them still believe that these birds of prey or 'raptors' as you call them are the natural enemies of game and should be controlled? That's what their father's might have thought, and certainly their grandfathers did in the days when many of the state actually paid bounties on hawks and owls."

"Yes, that's the sad part. It's a lack of knowledge. Times change, and I wonder if the misinformed hawk shooter still believes in such superstitions as hoop snakes or that a horsehair in the rain barrel turns into a worm," Dr. Meng said.

"Okay. But what about the goshawk I've seen in grouse covers? When I was a kid and we saw that big, long-tailed grey or sometimes brown hawk darting ahead of us, we usually picked up our dogs and went home. We figured there were no grouse when the hawks were there."

"You were wrong," said Dr. Meng. "I made studies of 14 nesting pairs of goshawks in New York and Pennsylvania. Their main food was red squirrels, chipmunks, and crows— three principal enemies of the ground-nesting grouse. I found, in fact, two nesting pairs in New York's Pharsalia Wildlife Management Area, and there were lots of grouse. The goshawk puts more grouse in the cover, not fewer."

Okay, Doc. We've got the word, and I for one plan to help spread it. Birds of prey are beneficial to the entire ecological system, and as Doc points out, since the Federal Migratory Bird Act also protects cardinals and robins, we might well ask the lawbreaking hawk-shooter, "Shot any cardinals lately?" And then, if we really have the necessary guts, shouldn't we turn them in? And that, my fellow hunters, is the real crunch.

Thank you again, Dr. Meng, for helping us all to put hawks back in the sky and keep them there.

38 LOOKS LIKE SNOW TONIGHT

IT looks like it's going to snow tonight. As I come into the quiet house it seems that I can almost hear my daughters, Maggie and Susan, when they were very young and trying to postpone going off to bed by saying, "Daddy, tell us about winter in the olden days."

Olden days? I was in my late twenties with a very short past, but to them I was the venerable sage. My wife, Ruby, often joined in, too, and told tales of her girlhood winters in the mountains of Montana. She liked to compare our eastern winters, where a few inches of snow paralyzed traffic and closed the schools, to the arctic blasts of Livingston, Montana. "And even when it was forty below zero, I bundled up and walked to school every day," she said. We were quite impressed until years later we all laughed to discover that her home was only half a block down the street from her school.

Frankly though, winters in the West and Midwest were and still are pretty rugged. Although the unyielding accuracy of weather bureau records probably won't back me up, it always seems as though it snowed harder, snowed longer, and snowed deeper when I was young. I can remember seeing the "lifelines" that ran from the house to the barn on South Dakota farms. In a bad storm you hooked your arm over the long rope and followed it to the barn and back to the house hanging on tight. Through the white fury of a Dakota prairie blizzard, failure to do this might mean that they would find you, along about May first, sitting up straight and dead in a thawing snow drift right in your own front yard. I often think about this when my snow blower won't start and a whole foot of snow menaces my garage doors.

And, incidentally, it doesn't really "snow" in a genuine   125

Dakota blizzard. It's like being stung with No. 2 chilled shot driven against your frozen face. For a long time we had a pair of big, black bearskin gauntlets that once belonged to my wife's father, Clair Flint. He carried these long-sleeved, furry gloves in his car during Montana winters in case he might have to use them to protect his face when walking away from a blizzard-bound car. I wonder what ever happened to those gauntlets. I could wear them out to the mailbox—after the driveway has been shovelled.

No doubt you've often seen pictures of those incredible herds of wintering elk driven down into the valleys of Montana and Wyoming by deep snow. How deep, you may ask? Well, we have a picture of Ruby in the "olden days" sitting on the top cross bars of a telephone pole sticking out a snow drift in Yellowstone Park. And to show her indifference as a true Montanan, she is calmly eating her lunch.

Have you ever noticed how deep the snow can get around a bunch of up-north hunters when the talk turns to the rigors of winters past? The first hunter to tell his tale of deep snow never has a chance. And so it was when my cousin, Gordon "Red" Cummings, joined the group. He usually waited until all the snow had fallen and all the tall tales were told. Then he produced a photo as a souvenir of a winter he spent as park engineer in Wyoming's Grand Teton National Park. One warm and sunny day in September he parked the family car behind his house in the town of Moose, Wyoming, and that night it started to snow. Somewhat later on in February of the following year, he was transferred East and his wife, Marlitta, took a picture of Red from the second story of their house walking around on the crusted snow in the back yard with a long stick, and probing deep trying to locate his car so that the Park Service rotary plow could come and dig him out. "When the snow covered the windows of the first floor we began to worry," Red said. "Tunneling out every morning was a real chore, and we had to be sure that we brought the snow shovels in the house every night or we'd really be in trouble. With the kids and all, one of our greatest fears was fire." Red and Marlitta are retired now and spend their winters in Fort Myers, Florida, where the snowfall is relatively light.

"Snowbound." What a reminiscent ring there is in that word. Do any of you "olden days" guys or girls remember how you had to memorize poems for school? I can still quote part of Whittier's "Snowbound." It went: "Shut in from all the world without, we sat the clean-winged hearth about, Content to let the north wind roar, in baffled rage at pane and door." And then something about "Blow high, blow low, not all its snow could quench our hearth-fire's ruddy glow." That was the poetic version of being snowbound, but do any of you big game hunters remember sitting red-eyed and shivering in a smoky, wet, cold tent way to hell and gone back in the mountains while the beautiful snow slowly covers the elk trails up to a horse's belly? You were running out of grub and beginning to wonder if you just shouldn't have been a stamp collector. According to a certain group of hunters I know, you must first be really snowbound in a leaky tent before you are qualified to complain about any phase of winter weather. Winter camping comfort has made some great strides, but it's far easier to fight the elements back home by turning up your electric blanket another notch after listening to storm warnings on the ten o'clock news. And yet I'll bet that there you are, back in the same tent with the same bad weather on its way next season. We never seem to learn.

Speaking of snow, one of the great myths of "winter in the woods" is the remarkable ease of travel in deep snow by that Ojibway Indian invention, the snowshoe. According to legend, these remarkable webs allow you to pad silently, swiftly, and with the greatest of ease over the deepest of snow. Don't you believe it. Based on my experience, the snowshoe is designed only for double-jointed acrobats and bearded Yukon trappers. Unless you were raised in the north woods and took your first steps on snowshoes at the cabin door, beware of long trips on these torturous devices. At first trial they seem easy enough as you throw your legs out to the side like a drunken duck to avoid stepping on your own feet. And then, as you waddle along, puffing and panting, you begin to realize that those long, seldom used muscles that run alongside your shin bones are beginning to come loose. If you remember the pain of "shinsplints" as a kid, you know what I mean.

Back in the "olden days" when I was a would-be trapper in northern Wisconsin, I well recall packing out a huge, at least 50 pound, beaver from Jones Creek three miles back to the main road on snowshoes. (That sentence looks like either the main road or the beaver was on snowshoes. But I was the one on snowshoes—and how.) It also looks like I'm out of space. If it snows tonight, we'll have a white Christmas. I hope you have a happy one, too, wherever you are.

HOUNDS, MULES, HELLDIVERS & ALARM CLOCKS
39

HOW many times have you read about the poor writer who sits sadly at his typewriter and stares at a blank white page waiting for a single idea to strike? My problem with this "Page" is just the opposite. I have too *many* ill-assorted items rattling around in my head or scrambled up here on the desk. What they lack is a theme—something to hold them all together and please my editor, who cares about such things. It's called "organization"—a virtue that often escapes me.

For example, how would you "organize" stories about a coon hound that can read, a mule that points quail, and how to hunt helldivers? Then I have a brand new bowhunting story. They can't be organized, so I'll just go ahead and tell them. If you insist, you can make up your own theme or rearrange them any way you want.

First, we have a letter from the Hatchie Bottoms at Bells, Tennessee, where Dave Brooks' friend, Ole Pete, was showing off his famous coon hound to a party of friends. The hound struck quickly, and as Dave says, "He led off down the way with that excited serenade." Well, pretty soon he got quiet. Not a sound. Ole Pete just re-lit his pipe and headed toward the dog's last announcement. His party began to doubt the hound and said so. Ole Pete paid no attention and just eased on his way. Well, after some minutes that hound took to singing out again. Those folks couldn't believe it. They asked Pete what had got into that crazy hound. Pete's calm explanation was, "Crossin' posted land." And then Dave adds, "You know, some folks who just don't *know* wouldn't believe some of these events." How true that is. In fact, there are some people who don't even know where the Hatchie Bottoms are. And another thing they don't recognize is the educational aspects of coon hunting gained entirely through travel. It always amazed me to find out how much ground a coon hunter can cover in one night. I once saw where an old hunter is reported to have said, "I've been further on a coon hunt than most folks have been on a train."

Mike Ryles, who runs a sporting goods store in Cuba, Missouri, wants me to know about Clark Farrar who lives about five miles above the Meramec River near Rattlesnake Hole in Crawford County. It seems that Clark has this bay mule named Bill who, Mike says, "points birds better than any pointer or setter that ever licked a pot." Word soon got out down there in the Missouri Ozarks about Clark's unusual mule, and two quail hunters who lived at St. Clair (that's near St. Louis) came on down and asked if they could see old Bill in action. As Mike tells it, "Clark, being very hospitable, grabbed a shotgun and away they went. Sure enough, in the first clover field old Bill pointed with his right front leg bent high and tail straight out. After downing a few birds they hunted several other places but with no luck. Finally one of the St. Clair boys suggested they try it over on government land. Clark hemmed and hawed about that suggestion, and when they persisted he finally turned around and said, "To get on government land we got to cross Benton Creek, and old Bill will quit us cold because he'd rather fish than hunt." (If you have any doubts about this one, you should know that Mike heard Clark tell it around the pot-bellied stove in Mike's own store. And that, of course, just about proves it—just about.)

If you are beginning to think that we deal only with stretching the truth on this page, let us turn now to an absolutely true story about Ollie Clark on the lake-filled prairies of northeastern South Dakota. Ollie was a highly regarded dining-car chef on the old Chicago, Milwaukee and St. Paul Railroad. Each fall he left his job to further pursue his art at my grandfather's duck hunting camp in Waubay, South Dakota. One fall day many years ago, Ollie decided to try the duck hunting himself, so my dad fixed him up with boots, hunting coat, shells, and gun. Ollie, an experienced rabbit hunter but with little knowledge of waterfowl, stalked the shore of the big lake and began to bang away at western grebe out on the lake. These "helldivers" 129 promptly dived and disappeared at the flash and sound of Ollie's gun. Finally out of shells, Ollie returned to camp where he met my dad. "Mister Mitchell," he said, "do ducks *sink?* Because, if they do, I've got the bottom of that lake paved with 'em."

Furthermore, if you also believe that this "Page" cannot recall anything that occurred after Custer's Last Stand and is completely unaware of the present, here's one that just happened. My young friend, Miley Bull, is a bowhunter, and this time of the year (it's November here now) he spends almost as much time in the trees as Robin Hood did waiting for the Sheriff of Nottingham. An avid and expert deer hunter, he is also a conscientious worker and parcels out his "off-the-job" hunting time carefully. So let him tell what happened the morning after he saw the giant buck at sundown just as he was leaving his tree stand.

"I was back there the next morning before going to work. Went up the same tree in the dark. A friend was going to pick me up at 8:30, and since my watch had been acting up, I had "borrowed" my wife's new travel clock and shoved it in my pocket. Just about 8:00, a doe and the big buck began to move down the trail towards my stand—the doe first, followed by the buck with his nose to the ground. At about 20 yards he passed behind a big oak, and I used that chance to come to a full draw on my bow. Just as he came back into view I anchored my bow string to my cheek and was telling myself "pick a spot" when suddenly out of my pants pocket my wife's alarm clock went off with a loud "Br-r-r-r-r!" I almost fell out of the tree slapping at my pocket—and I never saw those deer again."

Later on Miley's young and pretty wife, Cathy, told me that Miley had somehow lost her new alarm clock out of his pocket after the incident and then, wide-eyed, she said "Hey, should I *believe* that?"

"Yes, Cathy, you should," I answered.

As I walked away I wondered how far you could throw an alarm clock out of a tree.

Miley nailed a nice six-pointer three days later. Same stand, same tree—and you guessed it—no alarm clock.

40 JUST TAKE IT EASY

BILL TAYLOR had his own room with his own TV and many of the things he had managed to bring along when they closed up the old house. His daughter, Jan, couldn't have been kinder when she and Dr. John convinced him he should give up trying to live alone after Martha had gone and come live with her and her husband, Sam. Then, too, he hadn't been feeling so well, and Dr. John had told him that in addition to his arthritis he had high blood pressure. The doctor wanted him on daily medication, a special diet, and regular periods of rest with no strenuous activity of any kind.

"Maybe a short walk to the mailbox, but that's all for a while. I'll come see you on a regular basis."

House calls were rare things these days, but Bill had known John Casper Kimberley, M.D., when he was just a little shaver digging angle worms behind their chicken coop and a regular visitor on the back porch for a few of Martha's famous cookies. So Bill Taylor had become one of Dr. John's special patients.

Fortunately, Jan and Sam lived in an old remodeled farmhouse on the edge of town with plenty of room to breathe, and where you could see and feel the change of seasons. There was room, too, for Midge, Bill's old English setter, in one of the big runs built by the former owner of the farm. Although Midge once had the run of the Taylor house with her own box alongside the kitchen stove, she didn't seem to mind too much being relegated to outdoor living because of Jan's new wall-to-wall, cream-colored carpeting. Sam had rebuilt the old dog house, and Midge took to it readily. She did, however, spend a lot of time with her grey muzzle pressed against the wire fence, looking toward the house, waiting for Bill to come down on his cane to let her out so she could join him on the front porch where they both spent most of the day.

The doctor's orders on exercise weighed heavily on Bill because he had always been an active man in spite of the recent addition of the cane. And after Jan and Sam went off to their store in town, it got pretty lonesome. Most of his old friends were gone, and those who were still around couldn't get out to see him. "Without Midge," he often thought, "I think I'd just give up."

So the days rolled on for Bill Taylor until one sunny morning, after Jan and Sam had gone, he went down to let Midge out. To his amazement she bounced out through the gate and managed a few stiff-jointed frolics around his feet, almost knocking the cane out of his gnarled hand.

"What in the world has got into you, old girl?" Bill asked, peering down at her as his spectacles slid to the end of his nose. Midge, sitting at his feet, looked up at him with a new light in her faded eyes and suddenly barked. It was a puppy-like bark that seemed to surprise Midge as much as it did Bill. As they stood there regarding each other, a single yellow leaf drifted down from the big tree overhead. As Bill gazed up at the golden elm, he realized that fall had arrived, and it was hunting time again. Then they both heard it. A faint but clear "bob-bob-white" far off in a distant field. Bill cupped a hand to his ear and listened while Midge cocked her ears and matched his intensity.

"That does it," Bill said aloud, and started back to the house with Midge at his heels. Leaving the dog waiting on the porch, peering through the screen door, Bill made it slowly and quietly up the carpeted stairs to his room. He opened the closet door and felt around behind his clothes until he found it. The feel of the double-barrel through the heavy, oil-stained canvas case was like shaking the hand of an old friend as he pulled the Parker shotgun out of the closet. He checked the chambers, ran his hands lovingly along the cool, oily barrels, and smelled the unforgettable scent of Hoppe's No. 9. Putting on his tattered old hunting coat, which Jan had insisted on washing before he hung it in the closet, and his faded cap, he took a deep breath and mounted the gun to his thin shoulder. Somehow it had grown a little heavier, but it still felt good. He found half a box of old green paper quail loads in his drawer, spilled them into his coat pocket, and went down to join Midge, who almost fell backward down the steps in her enthusiastic greeting of Bill and his gun. Then he realized he had left his cane up in his room hanging on the doorknob. For a moment he stood there, feeling the old coat on his back, the old cap on his head. His legs felt stronger, and the pain in his shoulders had disappeared. He decided to leave his cane on the doorknob. He'd pick it up later.

And away they went, just a walk down to the mailbox, Bill rationalized, and maybe just a little beyond to the fields where the quail had called. They went slowly, just taking it easy, but with dignity and a certain determination.

About an hour later Bill and Midge were back at the house. Bill in his chair, dressed again in "civilian" clothes, with gun, coat, and cap back in the closet and his cane in hand. Midge was sleeping peacefully on the shady lawn at the foot of the steps. All was calm and quiet when Dr. John drove up.

"Glad to see you're both taking it easy," he said from his car.

Coming up on the porch with the stethoscope in his ears, he checked Bill's chest and nodded approvingly. Then he put the blood pressure cuff on Bill's skinny arm and pumped it up. Again he seemed pleased.

"Amazing. Those new pills are really working. Just keep taking it easy. See you next week," he said.

Turning to leave, he saw the three quail on the porch table. "Hey, what's this?" he asked. "Somebody been hunting?"

"Young Jim Stover just dropped 'em by. Take 'em with you. Probably not on my diet, anyway," said Bill.

"Thanks. I sure will. Long time since we've had quail for breakfast. Count them as my fee for today."

"It's a deal," smiled Bill. He knew full well how Martha felt about falsehoods, but this was such a small one.

Back in his car Dr. John called from the window, "Remember, just take it easy."

"You're the doctor," Bill answered as the car drove off. He winked at Midge, who raised her head slowly from the grass, and to this day Bill swears she winked back at him.